Where We Belong

CAROLINA
REBELS
SERIES

LINDSAY PAIGE

First Edition: February 2020
Library of Congress Cataloging-in-Publication Data

Paige, Lindsay
Where We Belong (a Carolina Rebels Series novel) – 1st ed
ISBN-13: 978-1-7325874-4-1

Collin

MY HEART CHARGES against my ribcage, needing and begging to escape and run free as I stand alone at center ice. Every single seat in the arena is full with angry fans, standing with their shaking fists in the air and screaming profanities to create the ultimate cacophony of static-like noise. I cover my ears with my gloved hands.

Why are they so pissed at me? What did I do?

My chest lifts a mile high with an inhale before deflating like a balloon, concaving my chest. The action repeats, over and over, faster and faster. Panic builds and builds with the screams of the fans. I want to move, get off the

1

ice, but my skates won't budge at all. It's like I'm part of the surface.

I need to get out of here.

The air that seemed to be in my lungs, allowing me to breathe, even if it is hyperventilating, suddenly disappears.

It's as if the fans steal every last molecule of my oxygen. My teammates now appear on the bench and they breathe my air too, sucking it right from me. Can't they see I need it? My hands claw at my throat, digging into my skin as if maybe I could break through to allow air in.

BUUUUUUUZZZZZZZZZ.

What is that loud noise?

BUUUUUUUZZZZZZZZZ.

Where is it coming from?

BUUUUUUUZZZZZZZZZ.

I need to BREATHE!

BUUUUUUUZZZZZZZZZ.

Gasping, I startle awake to the loud clunk of my phone hitting the floor. What the fuck? The red numbers on my alarm clock show it's three in the morning. I scoot over to the edge of the bed, lean down, and pick up my phone just as the call goes to voicemail. My heart, still clamoring to escape from my nightmare, triples its efforts upon seeing the missed call from Julie, my twin brother Cal's ex-girlfriend from high school.

Rubbing some sleep from my eyes, I call her back. She never calls this late. Something must be wrong. The ringing stops, but no one speaks on the other line.

"Julie?" I say. A choked sob sounds on the other side. I don't know why, but I automatically toss the covers aside and start dressing. As if she's nearby. As if I can go get her. As if I can rescue her from whatever mess she's in now. "Jules!" I snap as I slip a T-shirt on over my head, my phone now on my dresser on speaker.

"Can you come get me, Collin?"

"Fuck," I mutter. We're in two different states, twelve hours apart. I'd have to figure out how to go all the way to Florida, get her, and come back, all before practice tomorrow. There's no way to do it without missing practice.

"I'm in Wilmington," she adds, sounding almost hopeful.

I frown. "What?"

"Wilmington, North Carolina. I'm here. Please, Collin?" She's still crying, but she's desperate for my help now. "I can't…I need you to come get me. And don't tell anyone. Not even Cal."

"What's going on, Jules?"

"We don't have time for that right now," she snaps. "You need to pick me up."

"I'm grabbing my keys and putting on my shoes. Are you hurt? In danger?"

Julie doesn't answer me, which says enough. I lock my door and glance at the apartment door across the hall where my twin lives. We were going to live together when we started this journey of pro hockey together, but we needed the personal space. So, we live in the same building, same floor, and across the hall from one another. I only look for a moment before heading out.

Julie gives me the address for the airport by the time I'm in my car and I enter it into my vehicle's navigation system. Once I'm on the road toward I-40, I ask, "When the fuck are you telling me what is going on? What are you doing in Wilmington?"

"It's nothing, Collin," she answers with a sniffle. "It'll be bad enough when you get here," she adds in a quiet mutter, completely contradicting herself.

That sounds like it'll be a fucking disaster when I get there. "Okay. Fine. But you know I don't like walking into shit without knowing what to expect."

"I know and I'm sorry," she whispers. "But it's better this way, I think. Will you talk to me until you get here?"

"Of course." I catch her up on everything that's happened since I last spoke to her, which was only a week ago. There's mostly hockey updates, which aren't all that great for me, and then the anxiety updates—again, not all that great. I talk about Cal, running with a teammate and his girlfriend's dog in the mornings when we're home. I talk about small and stupid shit just to fill the silence. I've never talked so much in my life.

"Why didn't you fly into Raleigh?" I ask.

"I couldn't."

Her tone changes to one I can't quite understand or make out, but it's clear enough that I don't need to question her further.

She's standing outside as I pull up. My blood boils instantly upon seeing her and I suck in a breath at the sight of her beaten and battered face.

"What the fuck, Julie?" I demand to know the moment the door opens.

"Let's not talk about it right now," she replies as she climbs into my truck, tossing her luggage into my backseat.

That answer is two thousand percent unacceptable. "Who the fuck did this to you, Jules?" I reach out and let only the tips of my fingers graze her cheek. She flinches.

My anger flares higher at that. "What happened?"

"This isn't a parking space; we have to move."

"Jules," I whisper, heartbroken at the sight of my beautiful Julie, slumped over, scared, and refusing eye contact.

Finally, she looks at me. "I want to go to Raleigh with you." She grabs my hand and squeezes it with all her might. "Take me there, *please*, Collin." Tears well in her eyes.

"Okay, but this conversation isn't over."

Without letting go of her hand, I use my other to put the truck into drive and off we go. I want to ask questions. Lots of them. I don't want to assume anything, even though it's pretty obvious someone hit her. No, that isn't right. Someone beat the shit out of her. Julie opts not to speak. She stares out the window. I already have an anxiety problem and she's sending my panic through the fucking roof right now.

I don't like seeing her like this. I've known her for a long, long time. Cal and I met her when we were fourteen. That day isn't hard to remember at all. Whispers spread about a new girl all morning and that day in the cafeteria, I saw her. She was standing in line next to another girl, grabbing a carton of chocolate milk. I elbowed Cal in the gut to get his attention.

We were both a bit in love with her at that point, just from looking at her. She was a knockout even then. Before a word could be uttered between us, Cal took off to talk to her. We were all friends for a long while before Cal dated her, but he pursued her from the start. They broke up when we left town for college. It was mutual. High school sweethearts or not, neither wanted something long-term nor seemed to think they would last otherwise.

But Julie and I have always kept in touch. If Cal talks to her, he doesn't mention it, but I don't think he does. He left her behind just like everyone else. I told him once that I still spoke to her, back when we were in college; he thought it was crazy and didn't understand why I would keep in touch when he let her go. After that, I never talked about her or let him know when I saw her; Julie likes it that way too.

What will Cal think when he finds out Julie is in town and staying with me? Will he care? Will he be pissed? I know a lot about my twin, but Julie has always been a murky gray area. We fought over her before. Maybe that's not the right way to say it. Cal could be a jackass to her in high school and, well, I didn't always take his side. I didn't like taking sides, but if he asked, I took the side of the person who was in the right, or who was mostly right, and that wasn't always Cal. That caused a lot of arguments and tension between us because Cal thought I should choose him over her every fucking time no matter what.

"What are you doing?"

I glance over at Julie and realize I'm reaching for my phone. "Nothing." My hand retracts and rests on my thigh. "I was thinking about Cal."

"I don't want him to know I'm here, Collin."

"I can't hide you in my apartment forever, Jules. He pops in all the time." She sighs at this. "Why don't you want Cal to know?" This shouldn't be a big surprise to me. She never wants Cal to know and I never tell him when she's in town, but this is different. She's *hurt!*

She's silent for a minute, and I don't think she will answer, but as I park, she quietly says, "You two aren't identical to me, you know that, right?"

I swallow hard because it feels like she's somehow managed to punch me in the gut and allowed me to breathe. There's no time to dwell on what she's said. "Let's get inside. You probably want to rest."

Once inside, Julie climbs into my bed. She's visited before, so her comfort level in my apartment doesn't surprise me. There's always been a line with Julie. I don't cross it because she used to date my brother and I think it still exists. She sleeps in my bed and I take the couch.

My demon from hell roommate jumps onto the bed, causing Julie to gasp.

"You have a cat? When did you get him? Or her?"

"He's not my cat," I correct.

"Then what is he doing in your apartment?"

I walk over and sit on the bed, ignoring the orange tabby as he comes over to rub against my arm. "Because he won't leave. He somehow got into the building and ran into my apartment when the door was open. I tried seeing if he belonged to anyone, but no one claimed him. I leave the door open for him so he can wander out, but the bastard sits there and stares out into the hallway instead. He won't leave."

"And you don't have the heart to take him to the shelter," she adds what I left out.

"I took him to the vet and got him all checked out. They didn't believe me when I insisted he wasn't mine either. I'm not claiming him because I don't want him, but I'm not exactly going to make him homeless either." I hate the cat. I'm not a cat person, yet I don't have the heart to take him to the shelter, even so he can be adopted. It makes no sense to me, or Cal, that I kept this cat, especial-

7

ly since I always complain about him, but the cat likes me and I have a bad habit of petting him and scratching between his ears when he's around.

"What's his name?" Julie asks.

"He doesn't have a name because he's not my cat."

Julie laughs as I stand and walk over to my closet. "He needs a name. Can I name him?"

"Go ahead." She sounds like her normal self right now, and that makes me relax.

"He looks like a Marmalade to me. How does that sound, Marmalade?" Even I can hear him purring from way over here, but she's probably petting him or rubbing under his chin.

I glance at the two of them and am proven right. But that isn't what stops my lungs from working. Julie has unzipped her jacket. Her shirt is torn open and I spot more fresh bruises on her. She notices my staring. I can't even feel bad as she pulls her jacket tight against her, stands with her bag, and disappears into my bathroom to change.

What happened to her? Last I talked to her, she wasn't seeing anyone. Was this a random attack? Did she call the cops before she ran off? She shouldn't have run anyway. Julie stills my thoughts and my motions as I'm reaching for my extra sheets when, in a small voice, she asks, "Collin, will you stay in here tonight? I don't want to be alone."

"Uh, yeah." I close my closet door, walk over to the bedroom door, call for the cat to get out, and lock it on the off chance that Cal comes over in the morning. He has a key to my apartment, but not to my bedroom, obviously. I change my clothes, all the while freaking the fuck out over a new problem now.

I can't sleep in the same bed as Julie!

At this point in my life, I'm pretty sure I love this girl, but not only am I solidly in the friend zone, I don't know how to navigate the waters as far as my brother is concerned. And I have so much other shit in my head as far as my anxiety goes that this whole situation screams fucked up to me.

Julie lies on her side, facing me, while I lie on my back, staring at the ceiling because I don't know what else to do.

"You aren't okay, are you?"

"No," she whispers.

I take a deep breath. Fuck. "Will you tell me what happened?"

"I got caught up with the wrong person, that's all." She scoots closer to me and presses her face to my shoulder. "I don't want to talk about it," she mumbles. "Can we sleep now?"

"Yeah." That's not what I want to say, but I can't manage to say anything else as my arms snake around her. I hold her until she falls asleep. I don't know the full story, and hopefully, she'll tell me, but right now, I'm happy she's here and safe with me.

Unfortunately, I don't sleep at all. I'm too wired, too anxious, and too upset. To pass the time, I think about hockey. That normally relaxes me. It keeps my mind off of things with Julie, at least.

She eventually wiggles away from me, giving me much-needed space, especially for when I need to get up and get dressed.

"Collin! Get your sorry ass out of bed!"

Julie bolts upright in bed, looking terrified as hell.

"Go back to sleep. I'm locking this door behind me, so no worries. Don't open it for anyone but me, okay? I'll be back as soon as I can," I tell her.

The doorknob jiggles.

"Dude! Why is your door locked? Come on! We need to go!" He bangs on the door while I throw the blankets over Julie as she lies back down.

"Call me if you need me and I'll be here in ten minutes flat, no matter what."

She smiles. "Thanks, Collin. You're the best Kessy I know."

I grin. She used to tell me that, even when she was dating Cal. "I'm coming," I call as I walk to the door. I unlock it, but use my body to block his view because I know my brother. Just as I thought, he tries to peer inside.

"What the hell, Collin?"

"Back up and lower your fucking voice."

"Why don't you want me to—" His eyes widen. "There's a girl in there?" he whispers, all excited now. "Let me see her."

"Are you crazy?" I push him back and step out, locking the door from the inside right before I close it. "Let's go before we're late."

"Who's in there? When you'd meet her? Why are you holding out on me, Collin?"

I want to ignore his questions, but that will only make him crazier and more annoying. "She's just a booty call, but that doesn't mean she loses her privacy. Leave it alone. It's nothing."

He eyes me as if he knows I'm lying.

Hell, he's my identical twin brother. Of course he knows I'm lying.

Julie

I FALL BACK asleep after Collin leaves, but a knock on his bedroom door wakes me once more. I wait to hear Collin's voice. Instead, I hear Cal's.

"Baby? It's me. Open up."

What is that fool trying to pull? Most people can't tell them apart, but I've spent enough time with the two of them that I can tell the difference in their voices. Not to mention that Collin would never call me baby.

"Anyone in there?" he tries.

The doorknob jiggles and jiggles, and I start to worry. Cal wouldn't be so curious that he'd break into his brother's bedroom, would he?

"What the fuck are you doing, Cal?"

I fall back onto the bed with a sigh of relief.

"Just checking in on your booty call." I nearly snort at Collin's white lie to Cal. "Was going to see if she could tell us apart," he adds slightly quieter.

"Hand over my key." Oh, shit. Collin is pissed. Should I go out there, smooth things over? My stomach twists at the thought of facing Cal.

"What? Over a booty call?" The shock in his tone is more than my own shock over this turn of events. If he knew who was in here and how protective Collin is over me, he would be shocked from finding out, but not over his reaction.

"You were about to break into my room, Cal! There's a girl in there who needs some fucking privacy. You can barge into my apartment, but my bedroom is off fucking limits. Now, my apartment is off limits. Give me my fuck-ing key. You want to come over, you text first."

"Collin, you're being ridiculous. What's really going on here? Do you need a session or something?"

"Don't try and turn this around on me, Cal. This isn't about my fucked up life. Give me my key or I'll get it my damn self." Things are quiet for a moment and then I hear Collin say, "Now get the fuck out and don't apologize un-til you grow up and actually mean it."

"You're off your rocker today, man."

I wince. Collin doesn't like for people to think he's crazy or to call him crazy. Cal knows that. For his own brother to say that will hurt and nag him for a long time. I hear a door slam closed. For twenty minutes, I debate checking on him, but I don't want to crowd him after that either.

"Jules?"

I scramble off the bed to unlock the door for him. "I'm sorry, Collin. I didn't know what to do other than stay in here."

His eyes widen. "You knew it wasn't me?"

I roll my eyes. "I can tell the difference and even if I couldn't, you'd never call me baby."

He grimaces. He slowly reaches up and runs his fingers over my swollen and bruised face. "How are you feeling?"

"Blissfully in denial. I came to North Carolina to visit my long-time favorite Kessy, Collin. Everything has gone smoothly since the moment I stepped off the plane."

"Julie," he sighs.

"My face hurts; do you really want me to cry?"

His hand drops. "No. Are you hungry?"

"Yeah. I just woke up when Cal came over."

"I'm sorry I wasn't here. I stopped for groceries. C'mon."

I almost hesitate to leave the safety and security of his bedroom, but knowing he has his brother's key and that the door is most likely locked, along with the fact that I am indeed starving, helps move my feet to follow Collin across the apartment to the kitchen. He motions for me to sit on a stool at the bar while he cooks us up something. Marmalade meows and rubs against Collin's legs, walking back and forth between them.

"Are you ready to talk to me?" he asks.

I sigh. The answer is no. I haven't quite figured out a good lie to tell him. There's no way I'm telling Collin the truth. If I can't wrap my mind around it, how will he? I still have to tell him the big reason for my coming to North

Carolina: that I want to move in. Living back home isn't an option anymore. I can't go back without something like what happened last night happening again. If Collin says no, I'll hop on a plane and pick the next flight to a new home. Those are my two options: Live with Collin or move somewhere completely new.

My body hurts and aches, covered with a layer of bruises from my head to my toes, and it's because of something I've had no control over.

I flinch in surprise when Collin is suddenly next to me, grabbing me by the chin, but gently tilting my head back to look at him. "Stop blaming yourself," he says quietly. I wish I *could* blame myself. Then I'd know the hows, the whys, and the whens. I could take responsibility for it, but I can't. He's mistaking my confusion for self-blame. I yearn for that; it would be better than the turmoil of not knowing.

He looks hurt, undoubtedly because I flinched, but he caught me off guard. If there's one thing I've tried to learn, it's to be aware of my surroundings. Being unaware, even in so-called safe places, leads to bad things. I've learned my lesson. Collin leans forward an inch, stops as if he's hesitating, but then closes the distance to kiss my forehead. "Don't make me guilt trip it out of you," he mutters, his lips caressing my skin as he talks. And then, as suddenly as he appeared, he's gone and back to cooking.

"What do you mean?" Of course he wants to know, but that's not enough to guilt trip me into telling him what happened last night.

"My anxiety level is a thirteen, Jules. I've already had three panic attacks this morning, though I won't put the blame on you because things have been getting worse anyway." I watch the movement of his broad, broad shoulders as he shrugs. "You got me involved; I need to know."

Tears fall before I can stop them. Part of me wants to tell him. He's Collin. How can I not? But at the same time, I want to forget last night ever happened. A grilled cheese sandwich plops down on a paper towel in front of me and I smile.

"Your favorite comfort food," he says simply, wiping away my tears with his thumb. "Eat up." A moment later, he sits next to me with his own sandwich.

I come up with an easy, believable lie as quick as I can.

"It's partly my fault," I say, earning a disapproving glance from Collin. I take a deep breath. "I started seeing this guy and he wasn't who I thought he was. This," I point to my face, "is because I broke up with him." Less is more, right? And the fewer lies I tell, the less I have to remember. "Can I stay here for a while?" I don't want to jump in with the moving part. Collin is the only person to ever stick with me throughout my up-and-down, ultimately shitty life. I don't know what I'd do without him. However, if I jump in with both feet, he might suspect more than what I've told him.

He repeats the same thing he told me last night. "I can't keep you hidden forever."

"I know, but just for a little while? I can't deal with Cal on top of this."

His brother was fine in high school, but the older we get and the more I hear about him through Collin, he irritates me. Plus, if Collin is the best Kessy, then that makes Cal the worst in my eyes. I meant what I said when I told Collin that I can tell them apart and they aren't the same to me. I tell him every so often, but it's yet to get through to him, and for him to understand it's a good thing.

Cal is a sore subject for me ultimately because in a weird way, I feel like I was duped. Like I was with the wrong guy. I should have never hung out and fooled around with Cal in high school. All of it should've been with Collin, but I was too immature to see what really mattered back then. I think about Cal and feel nothing but regret. I'm in love with his brother, but we've been dancing to this song for so long, I'm not sure we'll ever be more.

Collin sighs and doesn't look so sure about keeping me a secret for a while.

"We never tell Cal when I'm in town. Why is this time different?" I ask.

"You're hurt, Jules," he says so simply, it's as if that explains everything.

It doesn't.

"Cal doesn't care if I'm hurt or not." And he wouldn't. I highly doubt that's changed about him from high school. Cal doesn't care because he doesn't care about *me*, not like Collin does. If Collin was hurt, it would be a different story because it's someone Cal cares about. Cal doesn't care about me. Therefore, so what if I'm hurt?

Collin doesn't acknowledge what I said. Instead, he says, "You know you can stay as long as you want. If you don't want Cal to know, then we won't tell him."

I throw my arms around him. "Thank you."

He holds me for a moment before releasing me. "Eat your sandwich, Jules."

After we're done with our sandwiches, there's banging on his door. "Come on, Collin! Stop ignoring me!" his brother shouts. "I'm sorry, okay? Give me my key back and let's move on. You aren't crazy, either. I shouldn't have said that." Collin turns to stone next to me, even though Cal is apologizing. "Please, Collin?"

"Go away, Cal!" Collin shouts.

"Is that girl still in there? Is that why you're being a dick to me?"

Collin sighs.

"Maybe you should talk to him," I suggest.

"Stay where you are." Collin stands and walks to the door, blocking it much like he did his bedroom door this morning, though there's no chance Cal can see me now. "Go the fuck away, Cal. Apology accepted. Happy? Now, go home. I need a nap."

"That girl is definitely still here. Why are you keeping secrets from me?"

"Because you tried breaking into my room this morning," Collin easily replies.

"I gave you an apology!"

"Which I accepted. That doesn't mean you get your key or that I'm letting you in," he fires back. "Now go home. You're seriously wearing me the fuck out." He closes and locks the door before Cal can argue with him.

"I'm sorry."

Collin frowns at me. "Why are you sorry? He does something stupid like that at least once a month." He sighs. "Do you mind if I actually take a nap? I promise to be better company later, but I'm exhausted."

I shake my head. He walks over to me and gives me the tightest hug he can without breaking a rib. "I'm glad you're here, Jules. I've missed you."

"I've missed you too," I whisper before he releases me and walks away to his bedroom. I just wish he loved me like I love him.

I'm lying on the couch, watching TV, when I hear gasping sounds from the bedroom. I shoot off the couch and see Collin lying on his back, his hands in fists by his side, and his chest moving rapidly with each inhale. He's told me he has nightmares where he's having a panic attack. Do they manifest themselves like this? He never said. No wonder he's getting more and more exhausted every day.

I rush to climb onto the bed and shake him awake. He startles and grabs my shoulders in a tight grip that has me wincing. His glazed eyes clear in about three seconds.

"Fuck, Julie! Are you okay? What's wrong?" His hands slide up and down my arms in a soothing motion.

"I'm fine," I say, causing him to frown in confusion. "You were almost to the point of hyperventilating in your sleep, so I woke you up."

His hands fall and he collapses back onto the bed. "Oh." He squeezes his eyes closed and tries to regain control of his breathing.

"Are you okay? Do you remember what the dream was about?"

"I don't want to talk about it."

"Okay." I hate feeling helpless when it comes to his anxiety. I never know how to help and not make it worse, or make sure I don't do something where he feels weak. But he looks like he needs a hug, so hopefully, he's okay with me shifting to lie on my side and throwing an arm around him in an one-armed hug. He's tense for a good moment, but then he relaxes and hugs me back with a deep breath.

"This hasn't been a warm welcome for you."

"I can't expect you to always get it right."

He laughs. "I'm glad you're here, Jules."

"There's no other place I'd rather be," I whisper. We enjoy some peace and quiet before I disturb it. "You're worse since the last time we talked."

"Don't worry. We're trying a change in medication."

"How are you feeling so far?"

"Like shit."

Despite the seriousness of the situation, I laugh a little. That's Collin's typical response when I ask after he's had to change his medication. "Does your brother know?"

"No," Collin answers quickly. "He worries about me enough. He doesn't need to know about this. Not to mention, he keeps pissing me off and…I don't know. I'm at this point where I don't want to tell him about these problems."

"You always have me," I say, lifting my head to look at him.

Collin smiles. "Thank god for that." The way he looks at me, as if he's actually thanking every God possible for my existence and the fact that he has me here, sucks all the air from my lungs and sends my heart into convulsions. The moment snaps in two when Collin looks up at the ceiling and asks, "I don't mean to bug you, but I want a more concrete answer."

"On what?" I ask.

"How long do you plan to stay?"

I hear the underlying questions. How long do I have to keep this secret from my brother? Will you answer me definitely to ease my mind, so I can stop worrying about it? With a sigh, I drop my bombshell. "Can't I move in?"

Collin frowns. He doesn't point out that this is a one-bedroom apartment or that definitely complicates the whole matter of me not liking his brother or how I didn't bring many clothes with me. Instead, he asks, "You don't want to go home?"

"Life sucks back home. I need a change. A fresh start. I'll only stay until I find a job and a place to rent. If you say no, I'll just stay in a hotel and burn through my savings. I can fly home, pack some things, and drive my car back. I'm not going back either way," I tell him.

His frown deepens. "What's going on at home?"

I rest my head on his shoulder. What isn't happening? "How do I get myself into these situations?" I whisper. It's like ever since my incident with Cal, I'm constantly running into bad luck head-on with no protective gear. "Maybe if I'm around you, I won't end up in sticky or stupid or bad situations."

"If you want to move here, you have my support, Jules. You're more than welcome to stay." He kisses the top of my head just as Marmalade jumps onto the bed. "I hate this fucking cat," he says as he walks up his chest and Collin scratches between his ears.

"I'd hate to know how you'd treat him if you loved him," I tease.

"Probably the same. Do you have a bathing suit with you?"

I prop myself up on my arm at his question. "Why?" The hotel I was going to stay at if my emergency plan of calling Collin failed had a pool, and in my frantic state, I grabbed a suit since I thought maybe I'd want to relax, but

Collin's question is coming from nowhere.

"I'm not relaxed enough. Do you?" When I nod, he says, "Then let's change."

My heart flips at the thought of seeing Collin shirtless. I don't know if I can handle what's planned, but I'm looking forward to finding out.

Collin

IT'S BEEN A long time since I've seen Julie in a biki-
ni. She may wear a frown and her arms may try their
best to hide her body due to the bruises blossoming
from that bastard she was with, but she's still beautiful.

"Here," I softly say as I hand Julie one of my hoodies
to wear on the walk down to the pool room. She slips it on
and I hand her a towel, which she wraps around her waist
to cover some of the bruises on her legs. I don't want to
think about how they got there.

Julie gives me a grateful smile before taking my hand.
"Lead the way."

As quietly as possible, I open and close my door. Our

footsteps are soft, but seemingly loud down the hallway. The last thing we want to do is give Cal a reason to pop his head out of his apartment. We make it down with no problem, thankfully. After shedding what clothes we wore, I pull Julie over to the hot tub. After turning it on and getting it going, we step in.

We both let out a contented sigh at the same time.

"What's your schedule looking like? I figured I could fly home next time you have to fly out," Julie says, resting her head on my shoulder.

"Game tomorrow night and we're flying out afterward because we have a game Saturday. So, you can leave Saturday, or wait a few more days because you'll basically have the whole week to do what you need to do."

"Okay. I'll look at flights tomorrow." She lifts her head and looks at me. "Have you dated anyone lately?"

I laugh. "When would I have time between panic attacks, hockey, my annoying brother, and you?" I touch the tip of her nose with that last part and smile. "I did go on a date for EJ not too long ago, but she's now his girlfriend."

"What? How'd that happen?"

"He was just trying to stay away from her because she was his nanny."

Julie nods in understanding. We're quiet for a bit, allowing the hot water to relax us, but then she says, "This may ruin everything, but I have to ask a question."

My hand moves underneath the water to gently grab her knee. "You can ask me anything."

"Have... Have you ever thought..." She turns toward me, her eyes crinkled with concern. Her mouth opens and closes. Before I can encourage her to ask me, she leans forward to place her lips upon mine.

Holy shit.

I grab her neck to hold her in place, kissing her like I've always dreamed of kissing her. Our mouths seem to be glued together as our tongues struggle for dominance. She straddles my lap, a strangled moan rocking through her. Just as my fingers dig into her neck, she's gone. My eyes pop open. We're both heavily breathing, but Julie has a wild look about her.

"I'm sorry. I wondered if you ever thought about that, about us. I shouldn't have." Her head shakes constantly as if she shouldn't have done what she just did. "Please tell me I didn't ruin what we have."

I hold my hand out. "C'mere." I can't believe this is actually happening. Did she seriously just kiss me? With a shaky hand, Julie places hers in mine and I bring her back next to me. "You haven't ruined anything. To answer your question, what if I say yes?"

Her eyes widen. "Are you saying yes?"

Instead of answering, I kiss her again, this time softer and slower. "Is that a good enough answer?" I ask.

"No."

I laugh.

"I've been thinking about this moment for years, Collin. I didn't think it would ever happen and I don't want to ruin our friendship, but I realized I can't live here without seeing if you feel the same way."

"I do." My voice seems to trail off.

"There's a but?" she asks incredulously.

"There are only two reasons I've never made a move on you: you're one of my closest friends and you used to date my brother."

Julie frowns. "Your brother has nothing to do with

this, Collin. He wouldn't care. That never should've happened anyway."

"I think it would matter," I disagree.

"I know you know your brother in ways I don't, but I know him in ways *you* don't, and trust me; he won't care. If anything, he'll think you deserve better," she finishes bitterly.

Better than Julie? I don't think a woman exists who is better than her. She's been with me through a lot of shit and she doesn't shy away when I'm going through my hard times. My brother can't always do that.

Julie grabs my hand, holding it hostage between both of hers. "What do you want to do, Collin? Date or forget this ever happened?" I open my mouth, but she places a finger over my lips before I can give her my answer. "If it's the first answer, you should know that I still don't want Cal to know I'm here. Not until we have to tell him."

My chest deflates. I don't understand why she has to be a secret. "Why?" I ask.

"That's a topic for another day."

I take a deep breath and nod. "Okay. Let's see what happens and we won't tell Cal until you're ready."

"Thank you." She kisses me softly and quickly before resting her head on my shoulder again.

"Are you sure you're ready for this?" I ask, thinking about why she's here to begin with.

"Yes," she answers without any hesitation. Before I can question her further, she moves on, clearly done discussing it. "When are we going on our first date?"

I smile. "It'll have to be next week after these road games are done with." The high over what's developed drifts away as I realize it shouldn't be so easy for Julie to pack up and leave Florida. "What about your job, Jules?"

"I don't have it anymore," she replies softly. "My boss started giving me a really hard time after I told him I wouldn't have an affair with him, so I quit."

"I'm sorry. What about your family? You want to just leave them behind?"

"I only talk to my parents and they know I'm not happy there."

"What about your sister?" I ask.

Julie sighs. "About a year ago, I caught her sleeping with my then-boyfriend. They are now married. I don't talk to her anymore."

"Fuck, Julie. Why didn't you tell me that?"

She laughs and lifts her head, moving away from me to the other side of the hot tub. "Because it was humiliating." Julie glides her hands over the top of the water. "It had been going on almost the entire time we were together." Her shoulders rise and fall. "It doesn't matter now anyway."

This happened while she was dating that guy, she obviously felt betrayed. "You don't think my brother won't feel betrayed when he finds out about us like you did when you found out about them, even if you two aren't together and it is years later?"

Julie shakes her head. "No, because Cal never cared about me." That can't be true. "Don't frown like that, Collin. He didn't. If you'd think about it, really think about it, you would realize that, too. How many times did you have to take my side and stand up for me because of how he treated me or because he was a jackass? Do you think he would've been that way had he cared?"

She may have a point there; I simply can't imagine

how he didn't see the most wonderful woman in front of him while he had her.

"Okay. I'll try not to worry about it. Let's head back up."

We get out of the hot tub, dry off, and make our way back to my apartment without running into Cal. I shoo Julie into the shower while I start dinner. Midway through, there's a knock on my door. I immediately sigh. There's only one person who would come to my door.

Just as before, I block his sight and refuse to let him in. "What do you want, Cal?" I ask.

He frowns. "Why are you being a little shit? I came to see if you wanted to eat with me."

"I already started cooking my own dinner; sorry."

He stands there, eyeing me as if he's trying to figure out what's going on. What's changed. I eye him and try to figure out how Julie can tell us apart. We don't have a tell. Our hair is the same, our faces are the same, and our voices are the same. We're exactly alike, yet we're not. Cal was born first. He was even born on a different day than me. He was born just before midnight on August twenty-third, while I was born shortly after midnight on the twenty-fourth. He's an inch taller than me and a pound heavier.

My nickname may be Thing One, but Cal is the best between the two of us. He doesn't have anything wrong with him. People say we're on an even playing field when it comes to hockey, but we both know he could best me. I struggle in life while Cal never has. There's no way I could play professionally if he wasn't by my side. The stress would weigh too heavily on my anxiety. I can't shoulder this life without him carrying half the load for me.

But Julie thinks I'm the best Kessy.

"What's up with you?" Cal asks, concern coloring his voice.

"Nothing. I'm fine. It's one of those days, I guess." He knows that's code for it being a rough mental health day.

Cal nods. "Okay. You rest and I'm next door if you need me."

When I return his nod, he crosses the hall to his apartment. I close and lock the door before returning to my dinner.

"Collin?"

I whirl around to find Julie. She wears pajama pants dotted with hearts and a tank top. "All done?"

"Yeah. Do you want to go? I can finish whatever you've started."

"Sure. Thanks." I walk up to her. At the last second, I decide to kiss her, but she laughs. "What?" I don't know if I should be smiling since she laughed when I kissed her, but she looks happy and that is reason enough to smile.

"I can't believe we can do that now."

"As far as I know, we're not; we're living in an alternate universe." Julie laughs. "Go keep an eye on my meal and don't let it burn."

We go our separate ways. Showers should be mundane or relaxing at best. But as I stand here, the water raining down on me, my anxiety slowly builds. My heartbeat steadily increases to a pace that is just fast enough to bother me and cause more anxiety. I take deep breaths as if that will slow my heartbeat. Is Julie really out there? Did we actually kiss and agree to date? And to keep this big secret from my twin brother? All while I'm struggling with hockey for like the first time ever? At least to the degree that I am.

Once again, I wonder why Julie thinks I'm the best Kessy. She wouldn't have these issues with Cal.

Things are mostly normal after my shower as we eat and watch TV. I pack for my upcoming trip while Julie looks up flights. Julie insists we sleep in the same bed again tonight. She cuddles against my side as I keep an arm around her.

"What if we don't work?" I ask one of the many questions boomeranging in my mind.

"We've been friends for this long. Do you really think we can't make it as a couple?" She lifts her head to look at me.

"You haven't worried about this?"

Julie shakes her head. "We're fantastic friends and I think because of that, we'll do our best to make it work. If it doesn't for some reason," she takes a steadying breath, "hopefully we can return to being friends."

I don't think either one of us wants to be without the other. She rests her head on my chest again and I take a deep breath, hoping sleep comes soon.

"You're the crazy one, you know?"

I look up to see my own brother. Or maybe it's simply me talking to myself. I can't even tell us apart right now. When I try to reach out to him, I realize I'm in a strait-jacket. "What the fuck?"

"I told you, you're the crazy one, Collin. This is where you'll be if you can't straighten up. How many more times will you score on us, huh? You're not helping any-one, brother."

I struggle in the jacket. "Let me out of this thing, Cal. I'm not crazy. I don't need to be in this."

Cal laughs. "You're with Julie now. You're definitely fucking crazy. If I'm too good to be with her, so are you. Not to mention, you keep having all of these panic attacks and she's not going to want you anyway. That 'best Kessy' bullshit is just that: bullshit."

My arms jerk from side to side as I struggle. I have to get out of this thing. My breathing turns to gasps as I feel trapped and the panic causes my skin to chill to an ungodly low temperature. I have to get out.

I have to get out!

Julie

CRUSHING PAIN WAKES me up. It takes me a second to realize I lie on top of Collin and his arms squeeze my torso so tightly, I can barely breathe. Damn, this hurts!

"Collin," I rasp, hoping to wake him up.

His cheek twitches and his arms tighten even more around me. He's going to break a rib or all of them if he keeps this up. Realizing my arm is free, I reach up and slap his face. His arms loosen, but his eyes don't open. Is he still asleep?

Just as I'm able to sit up and am about to call out his name again, I'm blindsided by a punch. The hit is so swift and hard that it knocks me off the bed, causing me to land on my shoulder.

"Fuck!" I hold a hand to my eye as I rock on the floor. The pain radiating from my eye, shoulder, and ribs is almost too much.

"Julie?" Collin crouches down next to me. "What happened? Did you fall?"

I shake my head. "You."

After a pause, his voice cracks. "I did this? Jesus." He carefully picks me up and sets me on the bed. "Do you want some ice?" I nod and he disappears. He soon returns with a bag of ice covered in a kitchen towel and gently sets it over my eye. "What happened, Julie?" he whispers.

"I woke up and you were squeezing the life out of me. I thought you were going to break my ribs. I slapped you to wake you up, but when I sat up, you punched me."

"I'm sorry. I'm so sorry. I was dreaming…" His voice trails off as he shakes his head. "I'm coming off of these meds. My dreams have been fucked ever since I started them. Are you okay? Is there anything else you need? How badly are you hurt?"

"I'm fine," I tell him. My eye hurts like a bitch, my ribs are a bit sore, and my shoulder doesn't feel all that great, but I'll survive. Guilt already consumes him based on the look in his eyes. I'm not about to make that worse by telling him how I really feel.

Collin leans forward and kisses my forehead with such care. "I'm sorry," he repeats. He shakes his head. "You didn't sign up for this."

"What do you mean?"

His muscles tense, his gaze moves to the door, and he quietly says, "Me when I'm off my rocker."

I really hate Cal. Lowering the ice, I reach out and grab Collin's chin, making him look at me. "You aren't off your rocker, Collin. You're a man going through a hard time. I signed up for whatever it's like to be with the best Kessy and I'm fully prepared to deal with that."

He stares at me for a moment. "Try to get some rest." He grabs a pillow and stands.

"What are you doing?"

"Sleeping on the couch," he says as if it's obvious. "I'm not putting you in danger anymore and it's obviously dangerous to share a bed with me."

It hurts that he doesn't feel as if it's safe to sleep in here with me, but at this point, I don't think I can argue with him. I almost want to, but I don't think he would change his mind. I smile a little, the best I can without it making my eye hurt worse, and watch him walk out of his bedroom.

I settle back into bed, letting the ice soothe my eye for a while, before finally going back to sleep.

When I wake up as the bed dips, I see Collin sitting next to me with a frown on his face. Marmalade sits next to him and Collin pets him, a constant purr coming from the cat because of it.

"I'm sorry, Jules."

"Stop apologizing to me. I'm fine."

"You haven't looked in the mirror yet. I'd feel better if you hit me back a few times."

I laugh. "I don't think I can do much damage." I sit up and reach for his hand. "Don't worry about it, Collin. You need to focus on the game tonight."

"I will when I need to. You're leaving tomorrow, right?" I nod, wondering how exactly that is going to work. "Are you seeing your parents while you're there?"

"Are you kidding me? When I look like this?" I joke, but it causes Collin to groan. "I might," I lie; I can't risk seeing them. "My lease is actually up soon and I'll get them to handle that for me. It came fully furnished, so I'll be able to pack fairly quickly and what I can't bring, my parents will store for me, I'm sure."

"I wish I could come with you to help." He sighs. "Do you want me to get someone to go with you? At least for company? It's a long drive back." Before I can tell him that I'll be fine, he says, "It'll make me feel better."

"Who would go with me?" There isn't any actual need, but maybe it's not the worst idea in the world. I also don't want him to worry about me unnecessarily.

"Deanna. She's the captain's girlfriend. They'll be able to keep it a secret, too," he adds as if he can see the question in my eyes. "Will you at least let me ask?"

I nod. "If it'll make you feel better and if she can keep it a secret, go ahead."

Collin smiles and leans forward to kiss the corner of my mouth. Butterflies explode in my stomach with that little action. "You can get some more sleep if you want. It's still pretty early. I'm heading over to Brayden's to run. I'll ask while I'm there. Go ahead and unpack what you have and make room for yourself today, okay?"

"Will do. Enjoy your run."

Those runs have been so important for him. If a person can burn off their anxiety by running, then that's what it does for Collin. It doesn't stay away, but he's calmer afterward and it sets his mood for the day. Running with that dog, Otis, does something different for him than working out with the team.

I don't know whether I should hope that Deanna can go with me or not. It'll ease whatever worries Collin has, but I'm perfectly okay going alone and driving that long drive back by myself. It'll help ensure I keep my own secret should anything happen while I'm down there. Marmalade climbs onto my chest, sits, and flicks his tail back and forth.

"Don't listen to what he says, Marmalade. He actually loves you." I scratch under his chin and receive a purr in response. "Okay, go away. I need a shower." He stares at me in defiance until I sit up and he reluctantly jumps off the bed, running into the living room.

After my shower, I unpack my suitcase and find a place to put some of my clothes. Collin returns from his run, smiling, because he convinced Deanna to go with me. He also called his psychiatrist, so he's on a new medication starting tomorrow. He gives me his brother's key, so I'll be able to get back into his apartment once I return.

The day passes without much incident and Saturday comes as well as a knock on Collin's door.

"It's Deanna," I hear from the other side.

I walk over and open the door for her. Her eyes widen at the side of me, looking rough with a big fat black eye. She would probably be more concerned if I wasn't wearing a long-sleeved shirt. "Hi," I finally say. "I'm sorry you're having to come with me." I step aside for her to come in.

"It's no problem. If Collin thinks you need company, I don't mind doing a favor for him. We need to leave soon, right?"

"Yeah. A car should be here any minute." I turn to grab my things, pet Marmalade one last time, and then we're out the door.

We don't say much as someone drives us to the airport, as we check in, and make our way through security. My phone dings with a text just as we sit down at our gate.

Collin: *Hey. How's it going?*

Me: *Fine. We're all settled in at the airport.*

Collin: *Good. I think you'll like Deanna, too. Thanks for letting her go with you. I feel better about it.*

Me: *She doesn't seem to mind that she's here. I guess I should talk to her instead of you. I'll let you know when we get there.*

"Collin checking in?" Deanna asks as she puts her own phone away.

"Yeah."

"Collin said he wanted Brayden and me to act as if this never happened. Is that because of whatever happened to you?" Her gaze lingers on my eye.

"Not exactly. I don't get along with Cal and I'd rather he not know I'm here."

"Oh, okay. So, Collin said we're packing you up because you're moving here."

I'm glad she's letting that topic go. "Yeah. I've had enough of Florida. I need something new and North Carolina is the place for me. I'm thankful Collin is letting me stay with him until I can get back on my feet."

"That's nice. I think you'll like it, and Collin seems like a nice guy. How do you know him?" she asks.

"I've known him since high school. I never lost touch with him. What's it like being a girlfriend to a pro hockey player?" I feel like I should get to know her as well. After all, we're spending this weekend together. I might as well get to know her to some extent.

Deanna smiles. "Well, I have a lot more girlfriends than I did before. I feel like I gained a second family. Like, take Collin for instance. We have an odd sort of friendship because he likes to run with my dog, so I see him most mornings. I also get to see what Brayden is like around kids because we sometimes babysit for EJ and his girlfriend, Raelynn. Don't get me wrong. I would still be with Brayden even if he wasn't a hockey player, but I like the life that comes with it—the people, I mean."

I nod in understanding, even though I haven't experienced that.

"Is there anything between you and Collin?" she asks curiously.

My mouth moves with a stutter of an answer, causing Deanna to laugh.

"Sorry. You don't have to finish answering me. Some of the spouses I'm around are kind of nosy, so I didn't think before I asked."

Thank goodness because I'm not sure how to answer that question right now. What I do learn about Deanna on our way to Florida is what she does for a living, more about the other spouses of some of Collin's teammates, and how she and Brayden met. The longer I spend time with her, the more comfortable I become. I tell her more about my friendship with Collin and even that I used to date Cal.

After picking up my car, we go to a local Japanese restaurant I never go to for something to eat. My phone rings.

"Hey, Collin," I answer.

"You didn't tell me you landed. Is everything going okay?" There's an edge in his voice, which has me worried.

"Yeah. We're grabbing something to eat before we go back to my apartment to pack. How are you doing today?" I ask.

"Not too good," he admits. His voice lowers. "Just took something to help calm me down, so hopefully that'll help. How's your eye?"

"Black."

Collin laughs. "I figured as much."

"I'm okay. Deanna is over here trying to be my new best friend," I say since she's subtly watching and listening. Collin chuckles. "I'm not too sure about her, though." Deanna laughs.

"She's good, Jules. I wouldn't have let her go with you if I thought she was a bad person."

"I know. You relax and we'll talk later, okay? Have a good game tonight, too."

"Thanks."

We hang up and I apologize to Deanna for being on the phone while we're at the table.

"Oh, don't worry. Sometimes, you just have to answer; I understand. Collin said something about how we might visit your parents. Are you planning to do that?"

Ugh. "They don't know I'm here, and I'd prefer to keep it that way." It may be February, but it's way warmer here in south Florida than it was in North Carolina. This hoodie has to go; I've been sweating for the past five minutes as it is and I can't take it anymore. I motion to my face and arms. "I don't really want to have to explain this to them."

"Oh, Julie," she whispers, her eyes on my arms. "I'm so sorry that happened to you. No wonder Collin didn't want you to be alone."

Can I just say that I love she didn't ask what happened or who did this? I relax in my seat, knowing that this trip will go just fine where she is concerned. I might even have a friend by the time I return to North Carolina. If only I can hurry and get back so I can stop looking over my shoulder every five seconds.

Collin

I BREATHE A sigh of relief when my skates hit the ice for my first shift of the night. Hockey has always been an outlet. It's a way to escape from my reality with anxiety and to work off the nerves. That probably doesn't make sense, but it does to me. Playing the game calms me down. It sends those nerves straight to hell so I can relax. It hasn't been like that lately, but tonight, it's like old times.

The panic from the past few days drains from my body with each stride down the ice. Passes to my brother are what reporters like to call magical and uncanny. But I love that when I make the pass, the puck actually goes to him and not the New York opponent. It's the simple things in life. Even the air in the arena seems to cleanse my lungs with every breath.

Everything seems to work for me in this game. My passes are complete. My energy level stays high. I even score a goal and get myself an assist. But something seems to change as the night winds down. It's like I'm at war with myself. I'm full of anxiety, yet I'm not. I'm on edge, yet I'm calm.

Cal throws an arm over my shoulder. "Want to check out the scenery? Grab something to eat?" he asks. We're not leaving until tomorrow, so we can go out and explore a little if we want.

I have no urge to open my mouth and respond to him verbally. Instead, I shake my head.

"You had a good game tonight." He continues walking toward the elevators with me.

I don't respond. I wish he wouldn't give me pats on the back like that. It makes me feel weak and pathetic that he feels as if he has to build me up and reassure me. It hasn't always been like that, but ever since my anxiety has trickled into my hockey life, he does things like this.

When I make it to my hotel room, I think about texting Julie to check in on her, but decide against it. If she spent the day packing, she's probably tired. I don't want to talk even through text either.

This weird restlessness stays with me as we travel. I dodge Julie's calls, but she texts me instead and those I answer, if only so she doesn't worry. She and Deanna drove home from Florida yesterday and she's working on unpacking today. If she isn't texting me about that, I'm getting pictures of the damn cat. Julie is having too much fun with Marmalade. Maybe if she moves out, she'll take the cat with her.

"What's going on with you?" Brayden asks as we stretch during warm-ups on the ice.

It's hard to stay as silent as I wish when people keep talking to me and ask questions that require more than a simple nod or shake of the head. I take a deep breath to gather the energy and will to answer him.

"Nothing's going on."

"Feeling okay?"

I nod, but he frowns. He leaves me alone and that's good enough for me. When we're on the bench after the first puck drop, I'm asked *again* if I feel okay. This time by Cal. He pointedly looks down at my legs, which are bouncing up and down. Leave it to my brother to notice a physical display of my anxiety. I nod that I'm fine and he frowns just like Brayden did.

Being on the ice doesn't calm me in the least today. My name should be Turnover Kessy. Or maybe Fucked Up Kessy. I certainly can't do anything right. My passes are sloppy. My legs move slower than they should. I'm lagging behind everyone like in a nightmare where you want to run as fast as you can, but for some reason, you're moving slower than a sloth. And do I have a bullseye on my back? Why the fuck do I keep getting hit? I can expect a few here and there, but this is getting out of hand.

Cal speaks to me between shifts, but his words bounce right off me. Whatever he's saying isn't important. Focusing on this game is important. Playing better than the shit I'm currently playing is important. Nothing else matters.

And then, it almost happens. It's late in the third and

we're tied at one. People stand in all different places around Savage and his blue paint. I'm to his left when the puck comes this way. It hits my skate and with horror, I watch it move in slow motion between the post and his skate, inching closer and closer to the red line.

No, this cannot happen to me again.

Savage realizes what's happening just as I reach out with my stick to attempt to bring it back toward me. He brings his arm back and covers the puck with his glove to get the whistle. The relief I expect to feel doesn't exist. I'm pissed the fuck off. Why does this shit keep happening to me? Why do I keep fucking up on the ice? I slam my stick against the boards and shove my brother away when he gets too close to me. All he will do is say shit I don't want to hear.

When I get back on the bench, Coach Mike grabs my shoulder and leans down. Before he can ask, I bark, "I'm fucking fine!" and yank my shoulder out of his hold. He probably doesn't believe me because I don't make it back on the ice, even when the game goes into overtime. That actually gives me relief. I can't mess up things for my team if I'm not on the ice.

Cal gives me some space afterward, thankfully, but I don't know what to feel when for our last road game, I discover I'm a healthy scratch. Should I be relieved? Or worried that my anxiety is about to get me kicked off the team? How did I get here? To where I'm watching Cal play without me? My entire team is down on the ice while I'm watching and it's because my coach doesn't have faith that I can play without screwing my team over.

This is the beginning of the end. First, I'm a healthy scratch. Then, they'll want me to take a maintenance day.

After that, they'll have it all figured out on how they can legally kick me off the team.

I should enjoy what time I have left, I guess.

"You've been quiet. Too quiet," Cal says as we walk toward our apartment doors.

I shrug. I still don't feel the need to speak.

"I'm worried, Collin."

"I'm fine."

"Yeah, that's what you keep saying, but I'm having a hard time believing you."

We've reached our apartments now. I don't know what he wants from me, but he obviously isn't going to get it. I turn away from him and insert a key into the lock. Cal gets the message and does the same. I spot Julie within seconds of entering my apartment, but Marmalade greets me first, rubbing against my legs as I close and lock the door.

Julie leaves the kitchen to rush over and hug me. "I'm glad you're back."

"What? You miss me?"

She laughs. "Of course I did. I'm fixing chicken Alfredo for lunch. Maybe you should put your things away and make sure I haven't completely taken over your bedroom." Her smile wobbles with worry.

Instead of responding, I kiss her temple and walk away from her. Her things are everywhere. It's almost overwhelming to see my apartment populated with things that are not mine, to realize that I no longer live alone.

While I like that Julie is here, right this very second, I wish she wasn't. All I want to do is fall face forward on my bed, cover my head with a pillow, and lie there until I decide to get up. Something tells me Julie will not accept that behavior.

I toss my bag near my closet, take a deep breath, and return to the kitchen where Julie places two plates on the bar. We sit down and begin to eat.

"I've been applying for jobs," Julie tells me.

"That's good."

"How—"

I hold up my hand. "If you're about to ask me how I'm doing, don't. I'm tired of that question." For the first time since we sat down, I look over at her. She seems worried now, but she nods. "Do you feel good about the move and everything? What did your parents say?"

Julie talks and I'm sure I hear what she says, but I don't process her words. I mostly asked so I wouldn't have to talk anyway. But then, Julie finishes her recap and asks me a question.

"You have the next week off, right? What are you going to do with your time?"

"Stay home. Some of the guys are going on vacation, but I'm not unnecessarily traveling during the season, even for vacation." Plus, I promised her a date. If this world loves me at all, I'll have enough energy and be in a decent enough mood to take her somewhere and make it enjoyable.

As we finish off our meal, she reaches over and rests her hand on my leg. "Do you know what I think we should do?"

Oh, fuck. I don't want to do anything.

"Be completely lazy today," she says.

I grin and lean over to kiss her softly. "I knew there was a reason I liked you."

Julie puts the dishes away while I sit on the couch. Marmalade sits on the back of the recliner and watches me with careful eyes. The fucking cat acts like he's the king of my apartment. As if the top of the recliner is his throne where he overlooks the kingdom of the living room, and Julie and I are his lowly subjects.

"Why are you glaring at Marmalade?" Julie asks with a laugh as she sits down next to me.

"Look at him. He's acting as if he owns this place. Maybe I should bring Otis over here. He might hate cats and decide to eat him."

Julie laughs as she backhands my stomach. "That's mean!"

"What's mean is a cat deciding to intrude in my home."

Julie chuckles as she shakes her head at me, but it makes me smile. My first true smile of the day. Julie takes control of the remote and for the rest of the day, we watch movies in blissful silence. She slowly moves closer and closer to me. Soon, we touch from shoulders down to our hips and down to our knees. I crack a smile when she not-so-casually yawns and lifts *my* arm to rest over her shoulders and dangle down her chest. She cuddles into my side.

"You've been quiet today," Julie comments that evening.

"Just that kind of day."

The best thing about Julie? She accepts this answer. She doesn't press for more. She doesn't complain or ask why. She doesn't try to change this fact. She simply accepts what's true and leaves it be. Now, she does say something, but I like what she says.

"If you need space or quiet or if I end up talking too much, tell me. I'd rather you tell me what you need than you be miserable or something."

"You're fine, Jules." She rests against me and I add, "For now," causing her to laugh.

I get up to feed Marmalade who whines like a baby when it's time for him to be fed. I often wonder who he whined to before he lived with me. If he lived on the street, did he still meow incessantly until he found food? When I return to the living room, Julie sits with her legs criss-crossed in front of her and a contemplating expression on her face.

"Do you think it'll feel odd to go on our date?" she asks as I sit next to her.

"Odd? No," I reply immediately. "Awkward at times, possibly. But we've gone out and done stuff together before. Only difference this time is we're calling it a date, I'll hold your hand, and there will be at least one kiss."

She reaches over to hold my hand in hers, resting them on her thigh, and smiles. "At least one?"

"Definitely."

"What if I want one now?"

I don't even get the chance to lean toward her before my phone rings. One look shows it's a call from Cal. For a second, I debate not answering. But if I don't, he'll only knock on my door and bother me that way.

"Hey," I answer.

"I can't remember. Are you taking me to the airport in the morning or am I using one of those car services?" he asks. Cal is one of those going on vacation.

47

"What time do you have to be at the airport?"

"Four thirty."

"I'm not getting up that early."

Cal laughs. "Fair enough. Are you sure you don't want to come with me? Or maybe go down and see Mom and Dad?"

"Right here is exactly where I want to be. You enjoy your trip. Maybe I'll pick you up when you get back," I tell him.

We talk for another minute or two and then hang up. I set my phone on the end table before facing Julie. Her eyes are back on the movie. That just won't do.

"Jules," I quietly say. She turns her head to look at me. Grasping her chin with two fingers, I lean over and kiss her like I've always dreamed of doing, but never have until now.

Julie

A GREAT KISS is something I've experienced before, but this touching of lips and tongues with Collin? Kiss is much too small of a word to describe it, and the pleasure coursing through my veins is like nothing I've ever felt. Collin and I? We were meant to be. That's the only explanation I have. Things were certainly never this...this... A moan pours from my throat as he forces me to lie back on the couch. Yeah, it was never like this with Cal. Or anyone else I've ever been with.

My fingers dig into the back of his neck as I hold onto him. Collin props himself up with one hand while killing me slowly. He grazes his fingertips over my collarbone, right above my sternum, and left to right, back and forth, just below my breasts so his knuckles brush across the undersides of my breasts. And I can feel every touch because I'm wearing only a thin sports bra.

Just when I suck in a breath from the feel of his hand, he kisses me harder. I'll gladly suffocate if it means kissing Collin until I pass out from lack of oxygen; it'd totally be worth it. A whiny sigh embarrasses me when Collin abandons my mouth for my neck.

"Jules?" he murmurs against my skin.

"Don't tell me you want to stop."

He lifts his head with the smile I'm most familiar with. "I don't want to rush this."

I nearly scoff, but refrain. In a way, it doesn't feel like rushing when I've been waiting *so* long for this moment. Collin has never led me astray, though. If it almost feels like we're rushing, then we should slow down.

His smile falters. "I need you to say something."

"You're also the smartest Kessy I know and I trust you." I lean up to kiss his cheek. A quick glance at the TV shows the credits rolling for our latest movie. "Let's watch one more movie and then go to bed."

Collin nods, sits up, and pulls me upright with him. Under his own accord, he puts his arm around me, making me smile. Marmalade jumps off of the chair and hops onto Collin's lap. He stares at Collin for all of three seconds before Collin huffs and pets him. I still don't think he actually dislikes the cat. And Marmalade obviously loves him.

We watch that last movie. We cuddle when we go to sleep. Sunday, we wake up and have a repeat of the day before. I'm a bit concerned. Well, I'm wondering if I should be. Even when I visit Collin talks more than he has been. Maybe he's tired from his trip and has to recharge before he's back to normal? I could be worrying for nothing, too. He's still functional. He cooks. He takes care of Marmalade. He told me we're going on our date.

The only problem is he's so quiet. He almost seems to be in another world, sometimes. Like he's not paying attention to this one at all. The last thing I want to do is bug him about it. We're on different terms now. Not to mention, I'm currently living with him. No way do I want to overstep or become a nuisance, especially this early on. My plan is to keep a watchful eye on him and if I feel the need to say something, I will. I'll have to hope that Collin won't nix me for it.

Now, it's Monday and we just left the apartment for our date. Collin hasn't said where we're going and I've decided not to ask. All I know is casual dress was the way to go. We're both wearing jeans and long-sleeved shirts. Collin has a hoodie on over his. I'm thankful I brought my jacket. It's going to be an adjustment living here. It's not easy going from warm Florida weather to forty degrees in North Carolina.

"I feel like a wimp," I say once Collin has parked and we get out of his car.

"Why?" he asks with a little chuckle.

"Because I'm clearly a Floridian. I need another jacket." I pull mine tighter around me.

Collin smiles as he takes my hand. "You'll get used to it like I did. We only have a short walk."

"Where are we going?"

"I know how you love museums, so we're going to an art museum."

51

"I can't believe you remember that." My parents are the reason I love to visit museums. That was essentially the biggest part of my childhood vacations and I fell in love with it. I still enjoy going, but it's been hard to make time for it the past few years.

Collin's voice softens as we walk into the building. "I remember everything about you."

And that is how our wonderful date begins. Collin holds my hand. He doesn't complain at my leisurely pace. He doesn't make a comment that we should hurry after we spend hours looking at various artworks. But once again, I worry because he's extra quiet. While this may not be his favorite place, I still thought he would talk to me more than he has.

"Collin?" He looks at me. "Are you okay? Truly okay?"

He quickly pulls me into a hug and holds me for a moment. "It's taking some time to adjust to this new medication. Don't worry about me yet." I relax into his hug, knowing he realizes I do have a reason for voicing my question. "I've been talking to you in my mind all day, but I don't feel like saying any of it. I'm sure I'll eventually tell you what I've been thinking."

"Okay." Even if he doesn't, it'll be fine. Collin is aware he's been quiet and that makes me feel better.

Collin smiles, releases me, and we finish our tour of the museum. I don't know what it is about visiting these places, but I always leave relaxed and fulfilled.

"Hungry?" Collin asks, and I nod. He drives us to downtown, parks, and we walk to a Mexican restaurant.

Things are still quiet, but at least now I know why. My feet tap to the music playing. I'm dying to make some kind of conversation, but I don't want to force him to talk if he's not in the mood. But I can always count on Collin to come through for me.

"We have all week to pretty much do whatever we want, you know," he says. "And we don't have to worry about Cal being around."

"Thank goodness for that," I mutter as I take a sip of my drink. "Is there anything you want to do while you're off?"

"Nothing in particular, but if there's something you want to do, we'll do it." Collin seems to study me for a moment and then he asks, "We don't have to talk about it if you don't want to, but am I missing something when it comes to you and Cal? I thought you both wanted to end the relationship."

"We did," I quickly say.

"Then why do I feel like there's some animosity toward him?"

Do I tell him the truth? Lying seems like a bad idea, and once Cal finds out, he'll discover the same from him, I'm sure. With a sigh, I reply, "That's because there is."

"But why?" he immediately asks.

My eyes roam around the restaurant. "If I tell you, it won't be here. We need privacy." At the mention of that, Collin frowns. "This isn't the place, Collin. I don't know if I want to tell you this, either," I admit. "I'm like a step away from hating your brother and I don't want you to feel the same way."

"How can you feel that way about him and not me? We're identical twins, Jules."

I reach across the table and rest my hand over his heart. "You're not the same in here."

It bugs the hell out of me that for some reason Collin thinks he and Cal are exactly the same. No matter how many times I tell him I notice the differences between the two of them, that they aren't alike to me, he doesn't seem to get they aren't the same. That he truly *is* the better Kessy. That he's his own person, not simply half of a set. But he never accepts what I tell him as the truth.

I pull my hand away as the waitress finally delivers our food. We're sucked back into silence while we eat. I can almost see the wheels in Collin's mind turning as he tries to figure out what his brother possibly could've done for me to feel the way I do about him. Telling Collin will be hard. Not only because of what happened, but because I know if Collin's heart is as good as it is, he won't be happy to hear what I have to say.

"I'm sorry." My gaze whips around from people-watching others in the restaurant to Collin as he says those two words. "This probably isn't the best first date you've been on."

"Don't be sorry, Collin. I'm with you and that in itself makes it the best first date." He doesn't seem to believe me, but it's true. "I've wanted this for a long time," I remind him.

"You don't have to lie to me. I'm not fragile."

"I'm not lying." And it pisses me off that he thinks I would. "And I know you're not fragile. You're the strongest person I know. I wouldn't lie to you."

He eyes me for a moment before smiling. "I'll lay it out there; you're the best woman I know."

I laugh. My heart warms at him turning what I always say to him around on me.

The waitress drops off the check and soon, we're in

the car on the way home. Collin ruins any chance of us waiting until we get back to return to the conversation about Cal, or even forgetting about it altogether.

"Tell me what happened," he quietly demands.

Whether it's support for me or him, I'm not sure, but I reach over and hold his hand in mine. With a deep breath, I begin my story. "About two weeks after we broke things off, I realized I was late. It terrified me and I knew if I was pregnant, it was Cal's." Collin's grip tightens. "I bought a test, but I didn't want to face the results alone, so I called Cal and asked him to come over."

"What happened?" he asks through a clenched jaw.

"He came over. I told him I was late and might be pregnant, that I wanted him to be there while I took the test." I take a steadying breath because what happened next is exactly why I can't stand Cal. "He told me he didn't care what the result was. He told me if it was positive, then I should get an abortion. He didn't want anything holding him back or complicating his road to playing professionally. He didn't want me riding his coattails and taking his money either. He repeated that he wanted me to get an abortion and left. I never heard from him again.

"I didn't see the point in reaching out to tell him that the test was negative and my period did come. He wouldn't have cared either way. To this day, he doesn't know whether I got an abortion or not." The fact an abortion was his gut reaction killed me. The fact he thought I wanted money out of him pissed me off.

"This explains so much," Collin whispers to himself.

"What do you mean?" I ask.

"This might be why he reacted the way he did when I first told him I was still talking to you. And why he always

55

seems extremely uncomfortable around babies. Maybe he regrets telling you that."

I can't help my scoff. "You have too much faith in Cal."

Collin shakes his head. "I can't believe he'd do that to you. And why wouldn't he tell me about it?"

The answer is obvious to me; I can't believe it's not to him. "Because he knows you'd kick his ass for what he did. You would've told him he didn't handle the situation well. You would've told him what you thought and Cal didn't want to hear it."

His voice softens and he glances over at me. "Why didn't you tell me?"

"I wanted to forget it happened and I didn't want you to think differently of your brother. It was obvious he didn't tell you, so I didn't tell you either."

His silence unnerves me more than before. He can't stay quiet now, not after a conversation like that. But Collin doesn't say a word until we're back inside the apartment. By that time, I'm good and nervous. He kicks off his shoes and plops down on the couch while I lag behind.

"Come sit with me, Jules," Collin says as Marmalade walks back and forth on his lap, leaning against his chest. I do as he wants. He pulls me into his side with one arm around my shoulders. "I'm trying to wrap my mind around it all."

"Want to talk out what you're thinking?"

"I'm pissed the fuck off that Cal would react that way to you. I mean, if he wanted nothing to do with the baby, fine, but he didn't have to respond the way he did." He sighs, his head falling back against the couch. "I keep picturing you standing there, worried and scared, and him walking out on you." He shakes his head. "No wonder you don't want anything to do with him."

"Well, it's over with now. When Cal does find out about us—"

"He can keep his fucking opinion to himself," Collin interrupts. He lifts his head to look at me. "All this time, I didn't have the kind of relationship with you that I wanted because of this crazy idea that somehow, whatever you had with Cal still mattered. I didn't want to cross some line. And it turns out that fucker screwed you over like that? All those times you told me he wouldn't care, I realize why you think that now. We should've gotten together a long time ago instead of dancing around this," he motions between us, "for all these years."

Collin nudges Marmalade off his lap and the cat meows in protest. He grabs my face and kisses me with a passion I didn't know existed. It's the kind of kiss that makes you react. My reaction is to crawl into his lap and pull his shirt off.

"We shouldn't rush, remember?" he reminds me as he kisses down my neck, his hands slipping underneath my shirt and tugging it higher and higher despite his words.

"We're not. We're catching up. Please, Collin."

That seems to completely break his resolve as he stands and carries me to his bedroom. We fall onto the bed together and Collin stops for a moment. His mouth parts, but no words are said. This moment feels impossibly huge and life-changing. The air we're breathing seems to be electric and on the verge of lifting us up to float around like it does. "I'm going to marry you one day, Julie." I don't know if I gasp or stop breathing altogether. "I don't want to fuck this up."

"You've never given up on me, and you've even res-cued me a few times. I won't give up on you. If we break, we'll figure out a way to put us back together and we'll be stronger. Let's focus on the here and now for the time be-ing." I wrap my arms around his neck. He allows me to bring those lips back to mine.

Tonight will officially change the dynamic of our re-lationship and I can't wait to experience every second of that change.

Collin

WAKING UP WITH a naked Julie sprawled over my body does crazy things to me. It's proof last night actually happened and I didn't dream up the best night of my life. Finally being with Julie was pure perfection. It was better than anything I've ever experienced. We fit together seamlessly. I could live off the memories of last night for the rest of my life and be as satisfied as a man could be without having the real thing.

Marmalade saunters into my room and jumps onto the bed. I might not like the cat, but there's something relaxing about him. As I scratch under his chin, Julie turns her head and kisses my chest.

"Morning, Collin."

"Good morning. Sleep well?"

"Yes. You?" She glances up at me with a bit of concern.

"No complaints from me. Are you hungry?"

"Let's stay here for a while longer." She manages to cuddle closer. "You seem very perky this morning." Her leg moves down slightly and bumps into my erection.

I laugh. "You aren't allowed to call my dick perky. It's offensive to all of mankind, and yes, that includes women." My hand leaves Marmalade to rest on Julie's thigh. "It seems unbelievable, doesn't it? That last night happened, we're both here and naked, and we're talking about my perky dick."

Julie laughs a little as she draws circles on my stomach. "It seems like the world finally righted itself and started turning in the right direction," she replies softly.

She's right. It feels like that. How can things finally be on the right track with Julie, but feel like they're fracturing when it comes to Cal? There are dozens of questions I want to ask him. Why didn't he tell me about what happened with her? Why did he do what he did? What else is he keeping from me?

Then again, I can't get too high and mighty in that respect. I don't tell him anything about Julie and he doesn't know about my latest medication change. The latter, however, isn't something he has to know. That's my decision to make. Which is probably what Cal thought. But if I thought I (almost) knocked a woman up, my brother would be the first to know.

"You were just a happy man," Julie says, lifting her head to look at me again. "What happened?"

"I was thinking about Cal." There's no reason to deny it, so I admit it.

"We're supposed to be free of him for a few days, remember?"

"Yeah, I know. I'm going to make breakfast." With a little bit of reluctance, I leave her in bed and hopefully, leave my thoughts behind as well. Getting out of bed is a bit of a bad idea, though. I want to crawl right back beneath my sheets instead of getting dressed and searching through my own fucking kitchen for what I need. "Jules!" I shout. "What the fuck have you done to my kitchen? I can't find anything!"

The irritation I feel right now is unreasonable. I know so, but controlling it feels beyond my reach. This new medication might not be a good fit, but I try to wait the full two weeks for it to get in my system good before saying anything. Unless I have a drastic reaction, of course. But wanting to slam cabinet doors closed and open drawers just to slam them closed again because my new lady is staying with me for a little while and has already fucked up my system sounds like an overreaction.

"What are you looking for?" Julie asks as she walks into the kitchen wearing some slinky-looking black robe.

"My little griddle. I want to make pancakes. I need my whisk too. Who gave you permission to rearrange my kitchen?" I snap.

She opens a cabinet I hadn't checked yet. "I didn't mean to," she replies softly, but firmly. "I forgot where things went and you weren't here for me to ask."

Fuck this. I'm not waiting my two full weeks. I haven't felt like myself since I started and it's obviously not helping me. Julie places everything I need on the counter.

She's about to walk away from me, but I grab her wrist and sigh. She's the last person who deserves to be treated the way I just treated her.

"I'm sorry, Jules. Will you get this started? I'm going to call my psychiatrist."

"Yeah, of course." She kisses the corner of my mouth and walks around me while I head to my room and close the door behind me.

A perk to being a pro athlete with an insane schedule is that I don't always need an appointment with my psychiatrist. He's an ass, though, and I say that in the nicest way possible. He already forced me to make an appointment to come in soon, but he's going to be adamant I come in now that I'm wanting yet another med change.

After waiting a few minutes, I'm able to talk to him and tell him what's been going on since I started the new medication.

"We'll try something else, but I want to see you this week," Dr. Gressley says.

"What the fuck for?"

"Because that's how these things are supposed to work and I happen to know you're on a bye week. I can tell a lot just by looking at you. You're making an appointment," he tells me.

"I look like shit because I feel like shit. You don't need to see me when I just told you and you'll make me come in after I've been on the new med for a month."

"If you want the prescription, you'll come in, and if you miss the appointment, I'll make a call to the team doctor."

See? He's an ass.

"I'll be there."

"Good. I'll transfer the call back to my receptionist and have the prescription called in within the hour."

I make the stupid appointment and then add it to my calendar with a reminder. The last thing I want to do is miss the appointment and have him reach out to the team. It's bad enough I have to see him when I do. Why I couldn't be like Cal in this respect and not have anything wrong with me, I don't know. What happened to being identical? Why was I the lucky one to be burdened with an anxiety disorder?

Sometimes, on the extremely hard days, I wonder how I'm supposed to live with this suffocating issue for the rest of my life. I don't know anyone else with this problem. How the fuck do they cope? *Is* there a way to cope? To manage this beast that doesn't want to be managed? It's like a wild horse that can't be tamed no matter how hard you try.

My shoulders cave forward as I realize that the rest of my life will be a series of some highs, hopefully with Julie, and some hard fucking lows, which will come more often than I'd like. The smell of bacon brings my mind fully to the woman in the kitchen. Sure, she knows some of what I go through because I'll talk about it with her. But she's never had to live with it. Does she know what she's getting herself into? What if it breaks our relationship in two because it's more than she can handle? Why didn't I think to warn her before last night?

I cover my face with my hands, my elbows propped on my knees, and try to remind myself that Julie isn't stupid. She had to have some idea of what she was walking into with me. If not, she got a good dose this morning with the kitchen fiasco.

There's a light knock on the bedroom door before Julie pushes it open. "Are you okay?"

I shrug. "Dr. Gressley wants me to come see him this week." She walks over, moves my arm, and sits on my lap. Her mouth opens, but I need to ask my question. "Do you know what you're getting into, Jules?"

Her brows pull together in confusion. "What do you mean?"

"With me." I swallow hard and force myself to add, "And my anxiety." She's silent for a moment too long. "It's different living with me and facing it instead of just talking to me a few times a week and hearing about it."

"I'm ready to face it, Collin. All I need is for you to talk to me and be honest about what you need from me. As long as we do that, I think we'll be okay."

Maybe she's right. I sure can hope so.

We spend all day at the apartment, with the exception of me having to pick up my new medication. When we watch the news at eleven, I realize today is Valentine's Day and apparently, it snowed this morning, though it was gone by noon.

"Did you know it was Valentine's Day?" I ask Julie, wondering if I should be in trouble for forgetting the holiday even though we're not even a week into dating.

She laughs. "Nope. Maybe we'll remember next year." Julie stands and holds her hands out for mine. "Let's go to bed." Her eyes twinkle with a mischievous glint. I happily follow her to my room.

The next day, we visit another museum. Julie enjoys herself. I wish I was at home. There's a layer of panic coated over my body, waiting for some stupid thing to happen and trigger an attack. Julie must be able to sense it, too. She keeps running her hand up and down my arm as if that will soothe me. If anything, it's reminding me that I'm ready to go nuts.

An attack doesn't happen, but being on edge all day wears me down and exhausts me to the point that when we get home, I go straight to bed.

Our break is officially over on Thursday. We have practice today and I have to see Dr. Gressley. When I see Cal, he glares at me.

"What the fuck, man? You were supposed to pick me up this morning."

"Sorry," I reply with absolutely no remorse. "I forgot to set my alarm and didn't hear my phone." Okay, so I heard it, but I was so fucking tired, I turned the ringer off. I knew he'd find his way home just fine.

He shakes his head, but looks around the dressing room as we change. "Hey, where's Marco and Scotty?"

I look around and notice that both of them are missing. Rams is the one who answers. "Lizzy went into labor last night and the excitement caused Sylvia to go into labor this morning when she demanded Scott take her to the hospital to see Lizzy and the twins." He sighs and shakes his head. "Be warned; Marco is going to be an absolute pain in the ass when he gets back tomorrow. He had to deliver the babies and he's already talking shit about it."

Holy shit. There are some things I know without a doubt I could never do. Delivering babies is one of those things. My anxiety would never allow me to be calm enough to do such a thing. I vaguely listen as Noah tells us we're more than welcome to stop by the hospital today if we wish to check in on them and see the new mini Rebels: Eric and Aubrey Polinski, and Seth Boyd.

All I want to do today is survive practice and my appointment with Dr. Gressley.

But practice doesn't go so well. I've never been more thankful to be on the ice and to not be playing a game. If this was a game, I'd be helping the other team more than my own. I don't understand why I'm falling apart. I'm doing everything I should. I haven't switched up anything in my routine to fuck with the superstitious gods. What in the ever-loving fuck am I doing to bring all this bad hockey juju down on me?

Frustrated and pissed, I leave practice for Dr. Gressley's in a superb mood. With a plain hoodie on, hood up, and a hat on, I also slip on a pair of sunglasses. One reason I hate visiting this place is because it makes me paranoid. I don't want any of the fans knowing what's wrong with me. I decide who knows about my anxiety and that's not some random Joe or Susie in a waiting room.

I always wear a hoodie, a hat, and sunglasses, even in the summer. I probably make others uncomfortable, but I don't care. Simply being in that room makes me uncomfortable; they should be too. Walking into the room tenses my muscles and urges me to walk right back out. But I take a steadying breath and walk up to the receptionist.

Instead of saying my name, I hand her my driver's license, just in case she doesn't realize it's me in my getup. No way am I risking my identity being discovered by saying my own name.

"It'll be a few minutes," she says.

"Thanks."

I take a seat far away from everyone else. The wait is excruciating. My head stays lowered, but my legs are constantly bouncing with anxiety and a sense of impatience.

The nurse finally opens the door, makes eye contact with me, and says, "Mr. Grey?"

I stand, thankful they always remember my request to use my middle name. Collin might be a common name, Kessy isn't as common, but I'm not risking them calling me by either in this building. She takes my vitals before leading me to Dr. Gressley's office. He stands and grins as he shakes my hand.

"How are you today, Mr. Grey?" He chuckles to himself. He thinks it's hilarious because of some book or movie or something like that.

"Shut the fuck up," I mumble as I sit down and take off my sunglasses and hat. "Why am I here?"

"I told you I wanted to see you and see how you're doing."

I hold my hands out. "So? How am I doing?"

"Are you still having nightmares and punching your girl in your sleep?" He seems to be analyzing me more than usual, and I don't like it.

"No."

"How is your sleep?"

"Fine."

"Anything you want to tell me that you haven't been telling me?" he asks with a raised brow.

"I don't lie to you," I snap.

Dr. Gressley shakes his head. "That's not what I said." When I don't say anything, he says, "You've been playing shit hockey ever since you scored on Liam Irving." I clench my jaw, but don't give in to his bait. "How's your relationship with your brother?" Without meaning to, I breathe heavily through my nose. "Not so hot, huh?" Dr. Gressley steeples his hands under his chin.

"I wanted to see you because I think you're spiraling. I've told you from day one that medication doesn't solve all your problems. It's not *the* fix. You've never seen a therapist, Collin, and I think it's time. I know—"

The chair screeches as I stand, slapping my hat back on my head and my sunglasses on as well. I turn and walk out.

"Wait! We're not done here!" Dr. Gressley comes after me, but I have a small head start and my legs are longer than his.

I rush to the door leading to the waiting room, burst through, and out the front door, running to my car once I'm outside.

Nope, nope, nope. I've gone this long without a fucking therapist and I can go longer without one. There might be something wrong with me, but I can manage it with a pill that works. That's all I need. I don't need to talk to some shrink, yet one more person who will know about my problems. I'm not fucking doing it.

I'm not even a half a mile away before my gasps for air turns into hyperventilating and I have to pull into a parking lot. I can't do it. Oh, god. What if he talks to the team and they force me? What if they keep benching me until I go? This is a damn disaster. But I don't want to go. I don't want to talk to someone I don't know about my problems. It's bad enough that I have to see Dr. Gressley so I can get my medication.

Pain blossoms in my chest as I try to figure out what to do. No matter what, I don't want to see a therapist.

Julie

I NEARLY SKIP around the apartment waiting for Collin to get home. My exciting news is dying to be told to someone and Collin is that person! But when he storms through the door, he rushes straight to his bedroom and slams the door behind him. What the hell? Do I go after him? Or would he rather be alone for a bit?

Marmalade stalks back and forth in front of his door, meowing and begging to be let in. Instinct tells me to wait. Collin knows I'm here. If he wanted my presence, he wouldn't have barricaded himself in his bedroom. I sit on the couch to wait him out.

An hour passes before he calmly opens his bedroom

door. He picks up Marmalade and walks over to sit next to me. He pets his cat and leans over to rest his head on my shoulder. We don't talk, though I am dying to ask him what happened. My instinct is still telling me to wait for him to come to me. Marmalade escapes after a little while and that's when Collin speaks.

"Sorry for all of this," he says with a sigh. "My psychiatrist wants me to see a therapist and I walked out on him."

I'm so confused by this. "But if he thinks you should and it will help, why not?"

He sits up and snaps at me, "I'm getting all the help I fucking need, Julie. It would be useless."

How is he getting all the help he needs if his psychiatrist thinks he should get more by seeing a therapist? I want to ask him, but this is obviously a touchy subject and I don't think my question would be appreciated. Collin continues to rant without prompt, however.

"I trust Dr. Gressley to do everything he can to keep my privacy. I know they are supposed to do that anyway, but he and his staff go the extra mile for me. How do I know a therapist would do the same?" He stands and paces. "Not to mention, I don't need to talk about nonsense to a stranger. I talk nonsense with you, with Cal, and even with Brayden sometimes. Why isn't that enough? I'm strong enough to get through this with only pills. Fuck him. He'll be lucky if I show up for the next appointment."

"But if Dr. Gressley recommends someone, then it'll be someone he trusts, right?" I can't help but voice.

Collin sends me a death glare. "I won't go to a therapist. I don't *need* it."

"Then why does he think you do?" I ask with honest

confusion.

His face pales as he glances away. "It doesn't matter what he thinks," he says after a long moment. "I know myself better than he does and that's not what I need."

Collin almost acts as if going to a therapist will do more harm than good. That doesn't seem to make sense, but I don't want to press him even further. He stalks away into the kitchen, ending the discussion. Do I still tell him my news? He seems so tense and troubled. I'll wait until he's in a better mood, when maybe he'll seem more like the Collin I know.

This side of him, the one who snaps at me and has anger stemming from his anxiety, isn't one I've had to face in person that often. It's a little startling, but exciting in an odd way. Collin is a reserved person in many ways; it takes a lot to see him act with such strong emotions. His anxiety seems to bring out a variety of his emotions that I don't see otherwise, not so boldly and simply present in a way that Collin isn't aware of.

When his anxiety attacks him, he's not as in control of his emotions. They get the best of him and it's so unusual to see Collin that way. It's much harder to watch him struggle when I can see it, instead of hearing his watered down updates. I can't help but wonder how long he's been getting worse; how long he's been giving me updates that sound like for the most part, he's doing okay. Now that I'm here, it's obvious he's struggling way more than he let on.

Collin fixes himself something to eat and then disappears into his room. My company is obviously unwanted tonight. I hate that because I'm here, he's holing up in his room. Maybe I should leave. I could always stay in a hotel to give him space. Maybe that's exactly what I should do.

When I knock softly on his door, he doesn't answer. He's asleep when I walk inside. Marmalade runs straight in and jumps onto the bed. He finds a spot near Collin to take a nap as well. After gathering a few clothes, I leave him a note next to his phone. He may sleep until morning, but he may not. Even if he does, he may want some space tomorrow.

"Jules?"

I stop at the door of his bedroom when I hear his voice and turn to face him. "Go back to sleep; I'm just leaving."

He frowns and runs a hand over his face as he sits up. "Leaving? Where? Why?"

"To a hotel to give you some space."

His brows pinch together in confusion, but silence stretches between us as I wait to see if he'll say anything. Time beats on until I turn to leave, a goodbye on my lips, and Collin finally speaks.

"Julie, wait. You don't have to leave. That's ridiculous." He huffs. "It's been a while since I've lived with someone and I'm having trouble dealing with that on top of this other stress. I normally come home to an empty apartment where I don't have to worry about putting up a good front or dealing with another person in general."

"That's why I wanted to leave. To give you space to deal with everything without me here." He doesn't need to explain anything to me because it makes sense already and I know it's probably hard on him.

Collin shakes his head. "I need to learn how to deal with it." He waves me over. I walk and sit on the edge of his bed next to him. He hugs me around the neck. "I'm sorry. Things are fucking hard right now."

"I know, but we'll get you through it. Do you want some good news?"

He pulls away. "Yeah, hit me with it. I always need good news."

I smile and take a deep breath. "I have two job interviews scheduled for next week."

A smile finally emerges from Collin, though it's not a full-blown one. "That's fantastic. Congrats, Julie. I'm sure you'll get an offer from one or both."

"Thanks."

"Unpack and I'll be better company."

Collin keeps his word for the rest of the night, too.

With my fingers all buttery and greasy, I reach for another handful of popcorn. Marmalade and I are watching the Rebels game. I don't know why I'm still eating popcorn. My stomach is a heavy boulder of nerves because Collin is not playing well. Aside from the fact that he's consistently having a string of not-so-great games, my concern is so great because of what this will do to him.

The broadcasters are brutal, too. Thank goodness Collin can't listen to them right now. They wish they knew the reason behind Collin's change in play. Why isn't he getting better? Maybe the coaches should make him healthy scratch more often because he's more of a hindrance.

I don't think Collin is *that* bad off, but I also hope I'm not wearing my rose-colored glasses as I watch him either. All I can do right now is stare at the TV and stuff my mouth with popcorn by the handful. Hopeful thoughts are sent out into the world every few seconds that Collin won't come home in too soured of a mood.

Unfortunately for all of the Rebels, they lose three to one.

Waiting around for Collin to come home sounds as exciting as twiddling my thumbs. Instead, I prepare for bed, climb in, and doze as I wait for him. Time passes without much notice until a door slamming wakes me up.

Oh, no. Not for a second night.

I sit up as he storms into the bedroom, barely glancing at me.

"Come here," I say as I pat the space next to me. Though there's no reason he shouldn't have heard me, he doesn't do as I asked. He yanks off his suit jacket and tosses it onto the floor. "Collin," I bite, raising my voice. "Come *here*."

The smallest of sighs leaves him. He kicks off his shoes and sits on the edge of the bed. I walk on my knees over to him, sitting behind him, and wrap my arms around his waist.

"Jules," he whispers.

"It'll get better," I remind him. "And I'm right here with you." My brain betrays me, thinking about how nice it is to be this close to him. "Can…" My voice dies. The idea I have might not be a good one.

"What?" Collin asks, turning to look at me.

"Do you want to end tonight on a high note?" I kiss him just once. "Think about something else for a while?" My hand eases its way down his stomach.

His eyes narrow. "You aren't just trying to cheer me up, are you?"

I smile. "That's the icing on the cake."

One second our eyes are locked and the next, Collin slams his lips to mine, turns his body, and pushes me back on the bed, earning us a hiss from an annoyed Marmalade who is booted from his seat. My fingers stumble as I work on his buttons. Collin doesn't seem to care about getting undressed at all. Not yet, at least. His hands clutch my waist in an almost uncomfortable grip, but his mouth…his mouth is heaven.

An embarrassing whimper jars against all the other sounds in the room and I'm a bit horrified when I realize it came from me when Collin pulled away. Collin grins, his face only a few inches from mine.

"We'll go out tomorrow, I promise. No matter how I'm feeling, we're getting out of here, okay?"

"If that's what you want." The last thing I want to do is push him when that isn't what he needs, or make him think he has to take me out all the time. All I've ever wanted from Collin was to be more than just friends with him. He's given me that already.

With my confirmation for tomorrow, he finally reaches for the hem of my shirt and yanks it off. The moments, sensations, and Collin in his entirety take me to a wonderful place, an unbelievable high that I've only ever had with him.

It's a relief when afterward, Collin falls asleep so quickly. I don't have to worry about him having trouble getting to sleep, but I pray he stays asleep throughout the night. A good night's rest has to make such a difference, especially in comparison to a lack of one. But as it turns out, I should've worried about myself because I'm the one who can't fall asleep.

The main thing on my mind is Cal finding out about us and how his reaction, whatever that may be, will affect Collin. I'm ninety-eight percent sure that seeing Cal and hearing whatever he may say won't affect me. But Cal has a *huge* influence over Collin whether either of them realize this or not. It doesn't help that Collin seems to think they are one and the same because they're identical. All I can do is hope Cal will think about his brother, and not his past with me, when he reacts.

Something warm keeps touching my skin, in various places, and my eyelids are like *hell no* when I think about opening them.

"Jules, wake up," Collin says in the sweetest voice I've ever heard.

"What time is it?"

"Eleven. Did I wear you out that much?" He chuckles, placing another kiss on my chest. My eyes rolling is enough of an answer for him. "Why don't you take a shower, get ready, and we'll go out for lunch," he suggests. "Besides, Cal doesn't believe I have a date today, so if I don't leave, he's going to annoy the hell out of me."

"You told him you had a date?" I ask, unsure about this simple development.

Collin lies next to me with his head on my pillow. "I had to tell him something, and he'll find out eventually. It's easy enough to get him used to the idea of me dating someone and thinking it's different than before, just because I'm not giving him any details."

I nod because I don't really want to make a big fuss. It's on the tip of my tongue to ask him how he's feeling today, but just by looking at him, it's clear he's feeling better than yesterday. Hearing him say so and confirm it would make me feel better, though. "I guess I should get my shower then."

An hour later, I'm surprised and slightly worried when we pull up at the ice rink complex. Collin wants to be here voluntarily after having so much trouble lately?

"It's chilly inside," he says. "I thought it might be a good way to acclimate you to the weather here while having fun." A bit of a crooked grin raises his lips. "Besides, it'll almost be like a trip down memory lane."

That's true. Collin, Cal, and I would also go ice skating together with some other friends before Cal and I started dating. Cal didn't have the patience to teach me how to skate, which should've been a sign, but Collin did.

We hold hands as we walk inside, rent skates, and Collin is impressed that I no longer need help tying my skates. Unlike back then, I see a different side of Collin. Despite his recent play, fans still support him, and those who are here skate up to him while we glide around the ice and ask for autographs.

Not only does he do that, but he has full-blown conversations with some of them. He truly makes them feel as if he's available to them and in no hurry to end the conversation, even though he's on a date. After each person leaves us, he glances at me with the cutest shy smile.

"You're amazing," I whisper after watching him spend twenty minutes talking to a kid and even showing her some stick handling skills with the stick he just signed for her.

Collin shrugs. "I'm just talking to people; it's something I do all day every day, unfortunately," he says with a bit of a laugh.

"But you don't have to."

Collin glances at me in surprise. "Yeah, I do," he replies seriously. "It's part of the job, and the fact that I don't want to be the reason anyone turns away from hockey. You don't think a quick conversation with a fan helps to further grow the game? That young girl? She'll probably play in the Olympics one day because she's dedicated already and wanting to learn, and hopefully by the time she's an adult, women's hockey will be even bigger than men's."

My eyebrows rise at hearing this. "You want the women to be more popular?"

Collin nods. "Or at the very least, just as popular. Within the next year, I want to start an organization or something geared just to girls and professional women's hockey. They should have the same chance as us."

Wow. "How come you're passionate about this?"

Again, he shrugs. "Met a girl in college. You remember me talking about Carla?" I nod. "She played on the women's team and we were friends." He stares ahead as his cheeks flush. "Dated for a bit. Anyway, she would always talk about how it would be so hard on her having a career doing the exact same thing I planned on having a career in, and it's always stayed with me how much that fucking sucks." His voice lowers in shame. "I just haven't gotten around to doing anything about it and I've decided it's time to stop wasting time."

"That's awesome, Collin."

"Not until I do something to help."

He's so amazing and I'm happy that he's mine. We can finally make an *us* possible, and maybe, just maybe, we can get our happily ever after.

Collin

MONDAY MORNING COMES as well as another practice. Another practice where my thoughts are so fragmented yet dominating, I have no clue what's happening. Well, that's not exactly true. I know based on the worried looks from the coaches and trainers and my teammates, even from my twin, that I am *not* doing well. I'm falling apart more and more and I don't know how to stop it. Hockey and playing professionally are supposed to be my safe haven.

My speed is like a turtle compared to everyone else's, despite the way my legs feel as if I'm pushing them to their absolute limit. When we practice shots, my aim…

well, I might as well not be aiming. Instead of feeling like I'm on a team, part of a team, I feel like a flailing six-year-old in the middle of a grown man's game.

What am I even doing here? Obviously I've lost my touch. I shouldn't be here. I don't know if I'd even qualify as an amateur hockey player, but I'm definitely not playing like a pro. Do you know what makes things even worse? One fucking mistake was all it took to unravel me. That's how weak and fragile I am.

I yank off my equipment and throw my ass into my stall, hunching over with my legs bouncing a mile a minute. I need to get out of here. I don't belong here anymore. I inhale, realizing it's loud even with my teammates talking, and still my lungs feel tight and restrained.

Fuck it.

I'm leaving.

I can't do this anymore.

I don't *want* to do this anymore.

I drown on air and my irrational thoughts sever the bits of sanity I cling to.

I stand and take two steps before a hand grabs my arm. Instinct has me yanking away and the built-up hysteria causes me to yell, "Get the fuck off me!" My chests labors heavily. It takes me a second to realize it's Brayden who stands before me with his hands up in surrender. "Leave me the fuck alone!" Every pair of eyes stares at me, but I don't care.

I need to leave.

I need to change.

I need to get away from these people and out of this building.

My feet carry me toward the door as I hear, "Collin,"

from a voice that sounds exactly like mine.

"Fuck off, Cal." I push through the double doors, relishing in the loud thunks as they close behind me. I head to the other locker room where our clothes are stored and quickly change, not caring that everything is being left in the wrong place. I'm in the corridor and almost to the exit when I hear my name again, but I know that voice too, and it forces me to stop and face Coach Mike.

"You don't need to leave, Collin." His voice scrapes down my skin in irritation with the caution and worry in it. "Not only because of the state you're in right now, but because we officially need a meeting."

Oh, fuck. This is it. They've decided I'm useless and no good. They're going to fire me. They'll null my contract, pack my bags, and kick my ass out of the building, forbidding me to ever return. I've fucked up too many times, have become too mentally unstable, and they don't want me around any longer. My anxiety swells like a tsunami in my chest, rising high above my six-two frame, and in seconds, crashes over me until I'm consumed with it.

Without a word, I turn and leave. I can kick myself out. Coach Mike calls after me, but I ignore him. My entire body feels like it's a small-scale earthquake, trembling and wrecking havoc. My hands shake as I reach into my pocket for my phone. I need Julie.

She answers on the second ring as I slide down in between two cars, my legs unable to keep me standing.

"Collin? Are you okay?"

I open my mouth, but I can't speak for breathing so hard.

"Collin, what's going on? Talk to me."

She needs to know they're firing me and that means

I'll lose my apartment and she'll have nowhere to stay and we'll both be homeless, but instead, I say, "Help me, Jules." I gulp in more of the cold air. "Fire me." Chills run down my cheeks, streaming straight from my eyes. "Breakdown."

"Collin, I don't understand. I need you to calm down, so you can talk to me."

Calm down? When the world is falling apart? When it's *my* world? A surge of anger rises and I throw my phone down on the pavement, busting it up. I can't do this anymore.

I can't do this anymore.

I can't do this.

I can't.

My energy crumbles as I fall over and curl into a ball, a darkness cloaking my mind and keeping me safe.

"It's okay, Collin. I'm here," I hear, but my mind is one big buzz of I CAN'T.

Over and over, those two words repeat themselves. I can't. I can't. I can't. *I can't* as I feel myself being pulled to stand. *I can't* as my face is grasped.

And then Julie slaps me twice.

The sting causes me to blink at her.

"Collin, I'm here," she reminds me. "It's okay. Talk to me."

Seeing her doesn't even relax me. It saddens me. I drop my head, my forehead resting against hers. She needs a strong man and look at me. Might as well get this over with.

"I fucked up and Coach wants a meeting. They probably want to fire me."

She takes one of my hands and holds it between hers.

"They won't," she says with such certainty. "I don't think they can, Collin. Not over this." Julie seems scared, but she takes a breath. "Let's go inside and find out what the meeting is about."

Oh, hell no. I shake my head. "I'm not going back in there."

"You won't be alone." She squeezes my hands, which shake like leaves in the wind. She gives them a tug and says, "Let's go."

Great. What other choice do I have now? I sigh, release her hands, and wrap one arm tightly around her neck to hold her close. Julie snakes her arms around my waist. The comfort I get from that makes me feel both strong and weak. Together, we walk back inside the building. It doesn't take long before we can hear the loud voices of the guys. What fun it'll be to face them after what I just did.

When I spot Cal, I remember who I'm with, her feelings, and everything that happened between them. I stop walking. Julie digs her nails into my side. The guys begin to notice us and eventually, so does Cal.

"Julie? What the fuck are you doing here?" Cal asks with a touch of accusation, his eyes roaming over every inch of the two of us. I can't tell if he's horrified, pissed, or both.

Coach Mike pokes his head out of his office, relieved to see me. "Collin, good. You're still here."

I focus on the most important thing right now, which is talking to Coach Mike.

"Who's Julie?" I hear Marco ask.

"My ex-girlfriend," Cal replies plainly.

The hallway is completely silent then, but it doesn't matter to us because we're in the office and Coach Mike closes the door behind us. He stands in front of us and holds his hand out to Julie.

"I'm Coach Mike."

"I'm Julie." She glances up at me. "Collin's best friend," she adds. I pull her closer, wondering why she didn't say girlfriend.

"Nice to meet you, Julie. Why don't you two have a seat?" He motions to a pair of seats while walking around to his own behind his desk.

Julie moves forward, but I yank her back to my side and shake my head. I'm barely in control here. I dip my head and very quietly whisper, "I can't let you go. You're the only thing that's holding me together."

"Okay." She nudges me with a hand on her back and I frown, but move forward. "Sit," she orders. After a moment of hesitation, I do and she follows, but she sits on the arm of the chair. All the while Coach has been watching us.

"How are you doing right now, Collin?" he asks. I simply shake my head. How could I express how I'm doing? And in a way that wouldn't freak him out? "Would it be correct to say you had a panic attack earlier?"

I nod and Julie chimes in with, "I think it would be safe to say he's either still in the middle of it or hasn't recovered from whatever happened earlier." She glances at me and all I can do is drop my head in shame. "Are you embarrassing him about his anxiety?" Julie suddenly demands to know.

"Excuse me?" Coach Mike replies with surprise.

It's nice she's concerned, but she doesn't need to accuse my coach of anything. "Jules," I say quietly. I squeeze her hip and shake my head to shut her up.

But that doesn't work. She lowers her voice and argues, "Collin, you're acting like you have something to be ashamed of. To be embarrassed about. You don't. You handle this the best way you can and you never act like this in front of me. What else am I supposed to think? They must be making you feel uncomfortable about it!"

We aren't doing this now. I need to know my future with the team. If there is one. Ignoring Julie, I ask Coach, "What did you want to meet about?"

Coach Mike eyes Julie for a moment, as if he wants to address what she said, but he decides to focus on me instead, thank god. "We've been talking and everyone agrees it would be best if you started seeing a therapist, two actually. One of your choice, for things away from work, and a sports psychologist, as your disorder never affected work until you scored on Savage in that game. If you'd like, you can also take a week or two off to decompress, recoup, whatever will help."

Thank fuck. They aren't firing me. That's all my mind hears right now. "Yes, sir," I automatically reply.

"Good. Do you want the time off?"

"Yes," Julie answers, causing me to jerk my head toward her. "Don't argue. You could use it and do you really want to deal with the stress hockey is obviously causing you while you deal with the stress of seeing two new people? If they're willing, take it, Collin. All you do at home is sleep because you're mentally exhausted." Fuck. I wince with the truth she's hitting me with and the fact that she's doing it in front of my coach. "You don't have to take the entire time off."

"But what's my reason? They have to report something."

85

"It's an undisclosed medical condition," Coach Mike says. "We can't use family as a reason when Cal won't be off too. But we can say it's medical, which it is, and we don't have to report anything more than that."

"I don't know." And I don't. This is starting to sound messy and complicated and bad.

"He's doing it," Julie confirms for me while I frown. "Is that all?"

"You're not making me look good, Jules," I mumble. She's sitting here, making my decisions for me as if I can't.

"It's okay, Collin. I'm glad you have someone other than your brother looking out for you. Go on home, rest, and we'll be in touch about the sports psychologist. Let us know when you've found your own therapist, or if you'd like us to help you with that as well."

Shit. Fuck, fuck, fuck. That's right. Part of this deal is seeing a therapist. Two motherfucking shrinks. I quickly thank Coach and stand to haul ass out of there.

Except Cal waits for us in the hallway. He is the last thing I need right now. Unfortunately, he doesn't get the memo.

"What the hell, Collin? What are you doing with her? Are you crazy?"

I snap.

I'm sick and fucking tired of him calling me crazy. I charge toward him, wrap my hand around his throat, and hold him against the wall. Julie makes some sort of protest, but my mind is fully on Cal right now.

"Don't you dare question me. Not after how you treated her."

"I don't know what you're talking about, Collin."

My hand tightens around his neck. "Don't fucking lie to me, Cal. You abandoned her when she needed you."

His eyes widen. "You know?" he wheezes.

"I know. Get off your fucking high horse, stay out of my life, and don't you dare call me crazy again." Finally, I release him. Without waiting for him to say anything to me, I take Julie's hand and walk out of there. He calls my name, but I ignore that too. Cal can go fuck himself.

Julie, thankfully, doesn't make a comment before we go our separate ways to drive home. I'm not a fan of this new development, but at least I still have my job. Dr. Gressley will be thrilled, I'm sure. I don't know how I'm going to do this. Talking to a stranger about my private life sounds impossible. Not to mention, I have my trust issues because I want to make sure this part of my life stays private.

My life is one huge clusterfuck right now when it should be such a happy time because Julie's here and we're testing out a relationship together. My sweet Julie holds her silence until we're inside my apartment. That's about as much as I can ask for.

"How are you feeling about what your coach said? Or is it still soaking in?"

"You should know I don't like it based on the other day," I point out as we sit on the couch. Marmalade saunters over and rubs against our legs.

"Can you tell me why, though?" she asks with genuine confusion.

I don't really want to, but I don't think I have a choice. "It scares the shit out of me, Jules," I admit. The woman has some patience today because she simply waits for me to explain. With a sigh, I turn my head to look at her as Marmalade jumps onto my lap for some head scratches. "When I see my psychiatrist, I always wear a hoodie, sunglasses, and a hat. They refer to me by my middle name because above all, I want my privacy super protected.

"I don't want a soul to know I go through this. I don't want the world to find out I struggle with this problem. And now, I'm supposed to go talk to a stranger about this? How can I trust them? How am I supposed to open up to them? What if I don't make any sense? It sounds like a pure fucking nightmare, Julie."

And it's a nightmare I'm about to walk through.

Julie

WITHOUT THINKING, I say the first thing that comes to mind: "Collin, quit whining and being a baby. The privacy thing you can set up, I'm sure, but the rest? That's all you worrying and finding excuses not to go for no actual good reason."

His eyes widen with shock.

"Collin?" Cal bangs on his apartment door. "Let me in! I'm sorry, okay? Let's talk."

Collin sighs. "Hold tight," he murmurs to me as he stands. He lets his brother in and Cal stops short upon seeing me.

"Why is she here?"

"She lives with me," Collin answers curtly, returning to my side, but still standing.

"Since when?"

"Since shortly after you tried to break into my room to get a look at her. What do you want to talk about?"

"Her!" Cal spits, flinging a pointed finger at me. The tension in the room thickens to the point where I don't know how I'm still able to breathe. Marmalade sits in my lap, keeping an eye on the twins. "I still don't understand this, Collin. It isn't like you to keep things from me and out of all the people you could date, you're picking a bitch like *her*?"

"She's the bitch? You're the dick who left her high and dry and *still* don't know if you have a kid somewhere out there?" Collin fires back. "What is wrong with you? How could you do that to someone?"

Cal laughs in a weird, non-humorous way. "Because I was eighteen and I definitely didn't want her in my life forever and I, like everyone else on the planet, wasn't ready for a kid! And we were about to go off to college. We had a plan, Collin. She would've fucked that up!" Cal yells. "Who knew if we could've stayed paired together if I had to worry about her and a baby? You wouldn't have this," he waves his arms around, "if it wasn't for me doing what I did! You need me to play hockey and you know it! It's in your fucking contract that we be on the same team!"

Whoa. Really? I know they are brothers, twins, but surely separation isn't impossible.

Collin is a stone for a moment. "You need me too, so don't throw that bullshit at me! You ask that they don't trade you without me. Ask her if you have a kid!" The two get closer and closer to one another and my worry about this escalating rises.

"I handle my shit the way I want, just like you do. Get off your fucking high horse and find some better pussy while you're at it. Maybe then you'll learn to stop whining and bitching about everything in your life. We have the same life, Collin!"

And the world explodes with his last words.

Collin throws a punch and within seconds, it's a bundle of bodies. They roll over the chair, bump into the coffee table, and all the while, fighting like they're teenagers again. Marmalade and I move to the kitchen. I know enough about these two that I don't waste my breath telling them to stop. Seeing them fight when we were teenagers was one thing; seeing them as full-grown men petrifies me.

There's so much muscle and strength. A load of anger and determination to win. Their hits are more accurate and their fury more reckless and dangerous.

They keep on until they knock over a lamp and Cal's nose is bloody.

They lie on the floor, breathing heavy, yet staying silent. Cal eventually takes his shirt off and holds it to his nose.

Finally, I ask, "Should I call your father?" He was always the peacemaker between the two. He helped settled arguments and told them what they needed to do or stop doing.

"No," they both answer.

"Are you sure? Because I think we should."

"Stay out of our shit, Julie," Cal snaps.

Collin elbows him. "Don't start. She's in my life whether you like it or not; find a way to be civil. If she can manage, you sure as hell can."

The room falls silent once more. Cal releases a long steady breath before turning to look at his brother.

"I'm sorry."

Collin nods. "Apology accepted." He goes to stand and that's when a bit of outrage emerges on Cal's face.

"That's it? You aren't going to apologize too?"

"For what?" Collin bites back.

"I said I was sorry because I was an ass and I know I give you a hard time when I shouldn't. Now, it's your turn to say sorry because you put us on such ridiculous pedestals and the world fucking falls apart if one of us falls off it. You're just as hard on me as you are on yourself, Collin. We both deserve a break. Now fucking apologize."

Collin glances at me, but I only shrug; I don't give a damn whether he does this or not. He also releases a long, steady breath, but his is much heavier. Loaded down with reluctance and probably a bit of shame, as if he thinks Cal is right. "I'm sorry," he replies quietly.

"Are you guys going to hug now?" I ask, earning glares from them both. "What? Your parents did in fact make you do that."

"If we're done, go home. It's been a long day," Collin tells Cal, ignoring what I said.

"You aren't going to tell me what happened?" Cal seems disappointed by this. Maybe worried too, but that doesn't surprise me.

"I'm taking a medical leave, essentially." Collin sits down on the couch and Marmalade claws his way out of my arms to run to him. "I have to see two therapists: one for hockey and one for all this other shit. I get at least two weeks. That's it."

Cal sticks his hands in his pockets as if he doesn't know what to do other than stand there and look awkward. "At least the team is working with you and trying to get you help."

"Yeah," is all Collin says.

His evil twin glances at me with uncertainty. But I don't want his help with anything, not even Collin. I can still see and feel his rigid back when Cal implied he was crazy. While knowing how Collin looks up to him and compares himself to Cal, there's no way I want to aid in enforcing that in any way. They need some separation and their differences need to be made more prominent. There has to be a way I can showcase that.

You've done enough damage here, I telepathically send to Cal. *Go crawl back into your hole and never come out, please and thank you. We don't need you. You aren't welcome.*

It's almost as if Cal can read my thoughts because his eyes harden and his mouth flattens as if to say back, *I'm not going anywhere. We're twins; we're inseparable.*

Ha. *We'll see about that.*

"Jules?"

My eyes snap over to Collin, who caught my silent conversation with Cal. The corners of his eyes are pinched with worry. "Yeah?" I ask.

"Maybe Cal should eat dinner with us?"

I glance over at Cal, who smirks. We totally had a telepathic conversation. Focusing back on Collin, all I say is, "If you want to." Of course, I don't want him here, but what can I do about that? He is easily going to be in my life forever because of Collin and I can be civil, even if it feels like it's against my own will.

Not to mention, after today, after seeing Collin curled like a baby on the pavement in between two cars, seemingly out of it and talking with such a bleak monotone that was so dreadful on my ears, I can do anything for him. Even his eyes seemed dead. Empty. Lifeless. And it's all because he thought he was losing hockey. His livelihood and career. Even now, his eyes aren't quite the same.

He seems to think about it for a moment, but then sighs. "Maybe tomorrow, Cal."

Without any hesitation, I walk over and open the door for him to leave. Collin shakes his head at me, but there's a barely-there smile on his face. Cal doesn't acknowledge me, except for the fact that he does leave.

"Jules, will you run and pick up dinner?"

"Absolutely. In the mood for anything?"

He shakes his head. After grabbing what I need to make my run, I kiss him softly and go on my way. I don't want to be gone long. I just run to the nearest restaurant, grab some grub, and head back. Unfortunately, Cal pokes his head out of his apartment as I'm walking to Collin's door.

"What do you want?" I ask.

"You will not come between me and my brother again, Julie. I don't know what you think you're doing here, but you will not ruin my relationship with Collin."

With a sweet smile, I reply, "You don't have to worry about me ruining your relationship with Collin. I'm sure you'll do that all on your own, Cal." I quickly enter the apartment to avoid further conversation.

Collin lies on the couch, knocked out from the mentally draining day, and Marmalade sits on the back of it, his tail swishing and flicking back and forth. I place our food on the kitchen bar, sit, and eat my meal. I won't wake him; he deserves to sleep. My concern for him has grown tenfold since this morning. He's in such serious trouble. Hopefully, the time off the team is giving him, plus seeing two therapists, will really help him.

After I eat, I curl up in his recliner and doze off. Who knew I would be as tired as Collin.

The sensation of being lifted wakes me.

"Just carrying you to bed," Collin whispers. "Thanks for supper."

"Any time." I nuzzle my face deeper into his neck, even as he lowers me to the bed.

He chuckles and manages to climb into bed without me having to move. "Don't start a war with him, Julie," he says with a bit of heaviness.

I lift my head. "Cal?"

He nods. "If he tries to stir shit up, or says something out of the way to you, don't say a word back to him." I open my mouth, ready to fire away, but he lays a finger over my lips. "No more glares either. Don't contribute to the war, Julie, because he'll make it one and then I'll be miserable."

"Okay," I reluctantly agree. He kisses my forehead in appreciation. "Can they really not trade one of you without the other?"

Collin seems a bit ashamed. "I really don't think I could handle a career like this unless I had him as backup, as support for my bad days."

Before I can stop myself, the words flow right out of my mouth. "Or maybe he's a crutch for you and you should have a tiny bit of separation."

"How about we let my shrinks figure that one out?"

The tips of his fingers drag along my side, causing a shiver to run down my spine. "It's been a long day; you're amazing; and I want to focus on the best part of my life right now: the fact that you're here." His mouth blazes a trail down my body until he reaches my sweetest spot. If pleasuring me is what Collin wants to focus on, I most certainly won't stop him.

The next morning, I shower and pick out the best clothes for my first interview. Collin isn't in his room when I come out of the bathroom, but I find him once I enter the main room. His eyes meet mine from across the room and he smiles hopefully.

Cal is here cooking breakfast.

Without skipping a beat, I walk confidently and comfortably over to Collin.

"Morning, Jules," he murmurs as he leans in and kisses me softly. "What time do you have to leave?"

"In about fifteen minutes," I answer, trying not to eye Cal. What is he doing over here already?

A plate clatters onto the bar in front of me, nearly sending eggs flying off the plate. "Eat before you go," Cal says blandly. He's made French toast, eggs, and bacon.

Collin grabs my hips and forces me to sit. "See? You two can get along just fine."

Except Cal is only doing this to wiggle his way back into Collin's good graces. It's not sincere. But I begin to eat because the twins watch and wait for me to do so.

"What's your job anyway?" Cal asks, apparently now

trying to make nice with chit-chat once everyone is eating.

"Dental hygienist."

He nods. Collin rests a hand on my thigh in approval. "Where is your interview?"

I give him the names of the two dental practices; it turns out one of them actually does dental work for the team. I wish I could work on Cal's mouth. Make him feel some pain.

We fall silent. Our forks clink and scrape loudly against our plates.

Suddenly, Cal breaks the silence. "Is there a kid?"

His expression is carefully blank. I can't believe he actually asked. Why not live on in ignorance for the rest of his life? Maybe it bothers him that he doesn't know because of what he did and if that's the case, I don't want to answer his question. The dark, still-angry part of me refuses to open my mouth to reply.

"No," Collin tells him. "False alarm."

The weight of not knowing lifts so visibly from Cal's entire being. Maybe there's a teeny tiny heart beating somewhere inside him after all. It's just buried underneath a load of bullshit and asshole behavior.

"Why didn't you tell me that?" Cal accuses.

"You walked out on me; you didn't care one way or another. Why would I tell you anything?" I snap.

Collin squeezes my thigh. "You know the truth now and it's in the past. Let's just move on," he says.

I'll have to work on that; I've been holding this grudge for so long against Cal, there's no telling how long it'll take to let it go. Standing, I tell him, "I need to go. I don't want to be late."

"Good luck," he replies with a smile.

Hopefully, I won't need any, but I'll always take some.

Collin

S ITTING AT HOME while Julie leaves for an interview and Cal leaves for practice is wrong. But this is where I am. I call Dr. Gressley for a referral to a shrink. His surprise and mild happiness irks me, but I let it slide. My livelihood is being threatened by my own mind. This morning, I woke up with a fierce determination that I wasn't losing hockey to this. I wouldn't lose my sanity to this. And I need to get myself together because I also won't lose Julie due to my mental issues, or even cause it to fuck things up.

I don't like the idea of therapy, mostly because it terrifies me to think of my mental health making headlines, of people discovering my struggle. Here I am, a professional athlete who is supposed to be a role model for kids. Kids who sometimes idolize us because they love what we do and they want to be like us.

How can I be comfortable with those same kids seeing me struggle with something they can't even see? That they probably don't understand. Hell, adults don't understand most of the time. They don't know what true anxiety is. They don't realize that I can't easily rid myself of it by thinking positively or breathing in fresh air. It's not a simple issue in any way, shape, or form.

The shame of having to deal with this, the fear of the public finding out, and the constant wondering of why only I struggle with it and not my twin plagues me daily. Would my teammates understand? Would the fans? Would I be ridiculed for something I struggle to control? Will they hear the word *disorder* or *mental health* and think I'm crazy? Unstable? Unfit to play hockey?

All I want is my privacy, and I threaten Dr. Gressley over how it must be protected at all costs with this new shrink. It takes him half an hour to book me an appointment for this afternoon with some guy named Trace Lexington. I'm already a little wary, considering the guy had an opening.

But when the time comes for my appointment, I'm right where I should be: in the waiting room. Ball cap pulled down low, hoodie up, sunglasses on, and a ball of anxiety tight in my stomach. I still don't want to do this, but I'm backed against a wall with no other options.

"Mr. Grey?"

With a small sigh of relief, I stand and follow the lady to an office.

I'm immediately unimpressed.

He's new. Boxes are stacked in the corners, one even on his bare desk. The man stands, slightly taller than me, and extends his hand.

"Sorry for the mess. I'm still settling in. It's nice to meet you, Collin."

"You too," I lie as he motions for me to have a seat.

It's then I notice he has one picture up on the shelves behind him. He, a woman, and two toddlers are at the arena, all wearing Rebels jerseys. Trace follows my gaze.

"My wife is a huge fan of the team. Being closer to the Rebels was one reason she didn't mind me accepting this job offer. I've already been told that we're getting season tickets next season." He shakes his head with a chuckle.

"Are you going to tell her about me?"

His expression turns serious. "Absolutely not. I take confidentiality seriously and Dr. Gressley informed me of how important your privacy is to you. I will not betray that, even to my wife." All I do is nod because I believe him. "Dr. Gressley also told me you've been adamant about not doing therapy and the only reason you're here now is because of the team forcing you."

"Dr. Gressley has a big mouth."

Trace smiles. "We're supposed to share some information with one another so we can better help you. Today, we'll just get to know each other a little better, okay? Relax. This won't be hard unless you make it, Collin."

He's already irritating me. "Do you even know what you're talking about? What makes you qualified to be my therapist? To be a therapist to anyone?" I ask, my anger shining through.

"Because we're alike," he answers simply. "I didn't want therapy either. I became a therapist specifically so I could handle my depression on my own. It didn't work." He shrugs as if he didn't just lay a bomb out there.

"Wait," I interrupt. "You're a therapist who needs a therapist?" This is fantastic. There's no way this will work. How is he supposed to help me if he doesn't have his own life together?

Trace shrugs. "We all need a little extra help sometimes, Collin. My point is I know what you're dealing with in more ways than you know. My wife struggles with some mental health issues too." He points to the photo behind him. "She had three panic attacks that night and the last thing I wanted to do was go to that game." They're smiling like it's the best night of their lives, though. "But we had the tickets. Our kids were excited about their first game, and we weren't letting them down. I know about pushing through, dealing with it, and being in a relationship during it all."

Now, I narrow my eyes at him. "Dr. Gressley told you about Julie."

Trace shakes his head. "Your coach did, actually. I called him prior to you coming to get his take on things. He said she seems to be a good rock for you. The relationship is new, isn't it?"

"Yes and no." Trace waits for me to expand on my answer and I do, telling him how we were friends first and about recent events. I even tell him the ordeal with my brother. "Julie is amazing; we're doing great."

"It's not stressful to be living with someone while you're dealing with this when you're used to being on your own?"

Trace better watch himself. Some of his questions almost make me feel like I'm doing something wrong. Or as if Julie isn't good for me.

"Yeah, it's stressful; she knows that. We're learning how to make it work. I'm not closing her out, but I'm taking space if I need to."

"That's good," he replies with approval. "Just be sure you're constantly talking her through it and that she knows what's going on and what you need. How are you feeling about this time off?"

My shoulders slump. "I hate it. Hockey is everything to me and now I don't have it because my head is fucked up. But I'll do whatever it takes to get it back."

The rest of my forty-five-minute session passes by like a quick breeze. I'm pretty surprised by the end of it. I didn't feel as if I was in therapy; for the most part, it felt as if I was simply having a conversation with someone. I even feel a little better as I leave, not that I'll ever tell anyone.

Well, maybe Julie.

Maybe this won't be so bad after all.

Maybe, just maybe, I can do this after all.

Julie perches on the edge of the couch when I walk into the apartment. Her face asks about thirty million questions while her mouth stays silent.

"How did the interview go?" I ask, sitting next to her. Marmalade jumps onto my lap, purring as he rubs against my chest.

"Fine. I'll hear back by the end of the week." Her eyes are wide as they watch me with so much interest and worry. I should end her suffering before she goes overboard.

"He's a Rebels fan," I blurt out. Okay. Not sure why I wanted to say that first, but okay. "His wife is a bigger fan, but they plan to get season tickets next year." Julie frowns. "What is it, Jules?"

"Is that what happened in therapy? You talked shop?"

"No." I shrug. "We talked a little about everything. It's just crazy that out of all the people who could be my therapist, it had to be a fan."

Julie watches me for a minute or so. "It went well, then?"

"As well as expected. I see him again next week." That answer does little to satisfy her. "I don't think I'll hate it, okay?" That's really what she wants to know. Whether this is something I might can deal with or something that will stress me out further.

She smiles wide. "Good. I'm happy to hear it." Julie snuggles into my side as close as she can possibly get. "Everything will work out. You'll feel better and be back on the team in no time."

Yeah, let's hope so.

"What are the guys on the team saying?" I ask later that night at dinner. Cal joined us, for better or for worse.

"Nothing."

My fork stops midway to my mouth. "Nothing? Nothing at all?"

"Nope."

That doesn't make any sense. Not after the ordeal my last day there.

"Hayes told everyone you needed time off for personal business and he'd cut the balls off of anyone who was gossiping or shit like that. I tried to joke that you were obviously the favorite and he even gave me a warning look. No one is willing to say shit because of him. I mean, I'm your brother and I've been banned."

"If only we could ban you completely," Julie grumbles.

"Now that was uncalled for," Cal objects.

I ignore them both. "Is it better or worse that he's being like that?" I ask Cal, who shrugs in return.

"Could be a good thing. He's made everyone realize that whatever it is, it's serious and not to be joked about. That will help when you get back and tell everyone why you were out."

"Who said I would be doing that?" The thought in itself horrifies me.

My stupid brother rolls his eyes. "I am. You can't miss all this time and expect the team not to ask questions. I think for trust reasons you should tell them. It won't be a big deal. And then, everyone can—"

"Can what? Watch me like a hawk to see when I'll break down next? I don't think so, Cal."

He levels a stare at me and I know he's about to challenge what I said. "What if the team makes you?"

"They can't. It's medical information; it's confidential." Thank god I have that going for me.

"Fine. What if they suggest it? You'll say no and leave the people we're closest to wondering what in the fuck happened with you? You're being selfish, Collin. The team can potentially help and be there for you and you're refusing based on your own pride."

Pride? He thinks this is about pride?

"It doesn't have anything to do with pride," Julie steps in. "Would you want me to share with your teammates how you abandoned me because you thought I was pregnant?" Cal's eyes widen and his jaw drops. "You didn't want a baby to interfere with hockey like Collin doesn't want his anxiety to do the same thing. You don't want your teammates to know what you did, based on your own *shame*, just like Collin doesn't want his teammates to know that he suffers. He thinks it is private, just like I bet that's what you think of that situation. He doesn't have to share if he doesn't want to and the last person who should be pressuring him is his own brother." She takes a bite out of a fry and ignores the stares from the both of us.

All I got out of that was the word shame. "I'm not ashamed." Julie rolls her eyes, causing me to look at my twin. "Right?"

"Do you think you could still be a role model to kids if they knew?" Julie asks before he can answer. "If the answer is no, then you're ashamed."

I could be a role model, but I don't know that I'd be a good one. Cal glances back and forth between us for a moment.

"She's a lot more vocal than I remember, and she was vocal before," he says as if she's no longer in the room with us.

"Perks of learning and growing after being treated like shit," Julie comments nonchalantly. She stands, takes all the empty dishes, and leaves us at the bar.

I watch her start a load of dishes, not really wanting to think about what she said. Any of it. If she's right, that's one more issue I need to work on and fix. I have enough problems as it is.

"The guys are getting together soon and I'm supposed to make sure you come."

Cal brings my attention back to him. "Just the team or family?"

"Family." His gaze drifts to Julie and he frowns. "Julie has already made headlines with the spouses and for some reason, they want to meet her. And Hook said he still expects to see you for the morning runs and workouts."

This is the part that sucks about taking time off without an actual injury. I still have to stay in the best shape as possible. There's nothing stopping me from being on the ice or working out. It would be stupid not to keep my body going as much as I can. But it'll be hard being with the team and not actually being with the team.

"A few of the guys said they'd come early or stay late to scrimmage with you on the ice to keep your legs somewhat fresh."

Julie suddenly whirls around, flinging suds off the dishrag she's holding, and throws her hands up. "Is this all y'all talk about? Hockey? All you're going to do is stress him out more, Cal. Surely y'all talk about something other than the game."

Cal and I exchange a look. Hockey is pretty much it for us these days.

"Unbelievable!" Julie throws the dishrag in the sink, sending water everywhere, and storms off to our bedroom.

"A lot more dramatic, too," he mutters.

I laugh. "She's stressed."

"Who isn't?"

"Everything okay?" I ask, wondering if I've been too caught up in my own life and missed something going on in Cal's.

He nods. "I'm heading home. Good luck with her." He nods toward my bedroom and off he goes.

I've survived my first official day without the team. That counts for something. I feel relatively okay about things, too.

Until I'm dumb enough to check the latest articles and see I'm one of the buzzing topics. Some folks run with what the team announced and leave it at that. Then, of course, there are the folks who insinuate this is something more. Something to do with my bad playing lately and the medical leave is an excuse to get me off the team for the time being.

And the comments.

Holy hell.

There are a bazillion too many fans happy that I won't be playing for the foreseeable future. I didn't realize it's been so bad that I'm getting that kind of hate.

"It's social media, Collin."

"Shit, Jules!" I exclaim as I nearly jump to the ceiling. "Did you really have to sneak up on me like that?"

"Are you seriously reading Facebook comments about yourself?" she retorts with a raised eyebrow. "Are you trying to upset yourself? People are downright hateful online and half of those people probably aren't even fans of the Rebels. This," she snatches the phone out of my hand, "is the last thing you need to do to yourself."

"I was curious," I explain.

"And then stupid once you started reading the comments. Social opinion isn't important."

"It is if Cal expects me to tell people about my problems. That will only get worse." I point to my phone. "I don't know if I could handle that, Jules."

She sighs, steps forward, and wraps her arms around my neck. "How about we focus on you getting better before you start contemplating opening yourself up to the team or the world?"

My face finds a comfy hiding place in the crook of her neck. That I'd rather do. I just need to slow myself down and focus on the most important thing right now, which is getting better in order to get back on the ice.

Julie

"**A**RE WE SURE I need to be here for this?" I ask as I look around the yard at the massive number of people. Honestly, I don't mind meeting people Collin is close to, but not only is this overwhelming, I don't know that I can live up to any expectations. Not Collin's or his friends'. This will be a disaster with my luck.

Collin chuckles as he squeezes my hand. "You seem worried."

Of course he would find this amusing. "You didn't answer my question."

"I'm sure, Jules. Relax, okay? The spouses will gobble you up like a hungry pack of wolves and then spit you back out to me."

My eyes widen as I turn to look up at him, causing him to laugh some more. "You're calling them wolves? Is that a sign? You know I'm a bad luck magnet, right? Maybe I should go back to Florida." Not that I'd ever go back.

His hand tightens and he yanks me against him, all the teasing gone from his eyes. "Don't say another word like that. You're supposed to be here with me."

His stare is hard, but brings me comfort with his seriousness, and the rest of his body is all inviting. The allure of his soul drags me even closer. Relaxes me. Soothes all of my ruffled, disarrayed feathers.

"Are y'all gonna get a room or join the party?" a woman asks, drawing our attention away from one another.

"Hey, Deanna."

I shake her hand and tell her hello. It's nice to see her again. A huge Rottweiler runs over and jumps up on Collin with a man following behind him.

"Down, Otis," Collin says. "Why am I the only one he does that to?"

"Because you let him," the man says. He extends a hand to me. "Brayden. Julie, right?" I nod. "Nice to meet you. If you need rescuing from the women," he nods toward Deanna, "be sure to let her know. She'll save you before anyone else will." Before I can ask how I'm supposed to tell her when I'll be surrounded, he adds, "Go on and introduce her before we're swarmed; I want to talk to Collin."

"But" I begin to protest. It's too late already. Deanna takes my hand and drags me away, while I look back at

Collin for help. He smiles! Brayden then blocks his view and I'm lost in a sea of men, kids, and food before finally arriving to where a group of women sit clustered together at a picnic table.

Some have really tiny babies in their arms. Some look on, gazing at the babies. Some immediately take notice of me and smile like a cat who caught a canary.

"What we need to know first," one holding a baby begins, "is how you went from Cal to Collin and," she wags her eyebrows, "are they truly identical?"

"Sylvia!" someone exclaims.

"We haven't even told her who we are!"

"That's too personal," someone else says.

"Why am I not surprised," another girl, to Deanna's right, says. "Hey, I'm Raelynn. I date EJ; I'm fairly new to the group, too."

They go around, telling me names I'm not sure I'll remember, and then Sylvia, the inappropriate one, goes, "Well?"

"She's nosy, likes to gossip, and just came off bedrest. You'll have to forgive her," a girl, whose name I think is Meredith, says. "You answer only what you want."

The women get quiet. They obviously want to me to say something. "They aren't identical," I finally say. They aren't the same; not in the way the woman wants to know and not in the way that matters. "I dated Cal in high school, a *long* time ago, and it was a mistake." Hopefully, I'm free to go, but when no one says anything else, I realize they want more. They're waiting and hanging on to whatever may come next. "There you go."

Their shoulders seem to sag in disappointment collectively.

"But Cal didn't know you and Collin were dating, right?"

"You really don't want me discussing this." Because how am I to keep my disdain for Cal out of my tone? I'm not an actress and I can't fake it. Not only that, but Cal wouldn't want me to and I actually don't want to either. As much as I wish everyone knew what an asshole Cal is, what happened was years ago and if these people love him, then that's their problem. Who am I to shine light on the darkness they are blind to?

"Oh, it sounds like we do," Sylvia nearly purrs with hunger for gossip in her eyes.

"Leave it alone," Deanna steps in, finally. "You don't want to push her away already, do you? If you traumatize her too soon, she won't ever come near us again."

Sylvia rolls her eyes. "Oh, whatever. You're still here and look at what you did to poor Zane. We immediately bombarded you about that."

Deanna stiffens next to me. "Don't go there, Sylvia. You're about two seconds from crossing a line and pissing me off."

The tension thickens quickly and heavily. Women glance at one another, waiting to see who will say something next and whether it'll break the ice or not.

"There are too many of you over here," a voice so like my favorite one appears next to me. Who knew Cal would be my saving grace? "You know when a bunch of women get together, a brawl is bound to break out, right?"

"I'm pretty sure that's not true," Raelynn says.

"If you say so. Julie, mind if I steal you away?"

"Not at all, Cal." I follow him away from the women,

grateful for Cal for the first time in probably forever. "Why are you being nice to me?" I ask once we reach a pair of coolers.

He opens one up and hands me a drink. "Because no one deserves whatever Sylvia wants out of them and Hook has Collin all tied up."

Glancing around, I don't even see Collin.

"They're inside, talking. I'm really doing this for him anyway. If you get upset, he'd be upset and it'd be a whole thing." He waves his hands around in the air. We fall silent, looking at the people, a good chunk of them watching us right back. "What did you tell them?" Cal eventually asks.

I turn my gaze on him. "About us?" He nods. "Is that all this is really about? You're worried about your reputation?"

"Yeah," he replies with a shrug of his shoulders. "These people don't mean shit to you, but they're family to Collin and me. Some more than others, but still. We're with these people more than anyone else and I don't want my past coming back and biting me in the ass because you want payback."

"Is that what you think? I don't want payback. If I could have Collin without you, I'd take up that offer in a heartbeat. Not just for me either. You aren't good for him and you don't even see it. If you care so much about what they think about you, maybe you should pay more attention to your damn brother and treat him better."

He opens his mouth, most likely to object to everything I just said, but I storm off. This will turn into a full-blown fight if I don't and that's the last thing we need here. I don't want to be around the women. I don't want to be around Cal. And Collin is being hogged by his team-mate.

With a sigh, I walk around to the front of the house and take a seat on the porch steps. It's quieter here. Nicer, too, since there's no one to bother me.

"Hey, are you okay?" a male voice asks.

I look up from my shoes to see a young couple and two kids. "Yeah, I'm fine. Just needed a break." I give my best reassuring smile.

"You must be Collin's girlfriend. Sylvia got to you, didn't she?" the girl asks with a shake of her head.

"Where's Collin?" the guy asks.

"Brayden has him in the house somewhere."

The guy transfers the little girl to her mom and bounds up the stairs. The woman sits next to me with the girl resting on her knees and the baby nestled against her chest, asleep.

"I'm Sydney. That was my husband, Ian. This is my little girl, Savannah, and my baby boy, Andrew. He'll get Collin for you. I hope they weren't too bad. I know it can be hard meeting the spouses for the first time, especially if your situation is anything but ideal. They mean well, they really do, but it's a hectic time and they often forget their manners. The best thing for you to do is find your voice. Learn how to tell them to back off." She shrugs. "It's helped me."

"Telling them to back off is smart?" I ask with sur-prise. I wouldn't think they would like that.

Sydney laughs a little. "Sylvia has no boundaries, so if you don't want her in your relationship entirely, you have to tell her to butt out. It's the only way to stop her. She will respect your wishes, but only if you make them known. Otherwise, it's free game."

"Jules," I hear my favorite voice along with a few sets of footsteps. "They ran you off already?" he asks with disappointment.

"Pretty much," Sydney answers for me. "You shouldn't have left her."

"It's okay," I quickly say, standing and plastering on a smile. I don't want Collin worrying about me right now. Not with this. "We should get back to the party."

Collin eyes me carefully before holding out his hand. "Do you want to go home or head back out?"

"They didn't scare me off." That's the truth. It's also the absolute right answer because Collin grins before tugging me through the house and back to the swarm of people.

It seems the women aren't congregated together anymore. Not without their men by their sides at least. When we approach the group I not long ago left, the man with Sylvia speaks to me.

"She's uncontrollable a lot of the time, but she's worse right now from where she was on bedrest. Ignore her or tell her to shut up; she won't be offended."

I glance at Sylvia who nods and shrugs.

"There's only one question we're all dying to ask you now."

Great. I'm still the topic of discussion. "What is it?"

"How did you know it was Cal and not Collin a while ago?"

Collin looks at me with a curious expression, obviously having no idea that I've interacted with his brother. I mock Sylvia's shrug and reply, "I told you they aren't identical."

They all stare at me dumbfounded now. I'm telling them identical twins aren't identical and they don't understand how. That's not my problem, though.

"How can you easily tell them apart?" Brayden asks with genuine curiosity.

"Spend enough time with them and it's easy."

"How are we different?" Cal asks, catching onto our conversation and sitting on the edge of the table. His eyes hold a bit of a challenge, but his tone tells me he doesn't care about this answer at all. His brother, on the other hand, stands next to me with bated breath.

"Aside from physically?" I perk an eyebrow and smile because I know the girls already think one of them is different than the other in this particular area. Cal stares and waits. "There are subtle but obvious differences, even in your voices. For example, if I was behind a closed door and you tried to get me to open it, pretending to be Collin, I can tell it's you by your voice. Not just based on how you talk to me."

Cal's eyes squint a little, but Collin chuckles. "And one of you obviously has a better personality."

The people at the picnic tables laugh. Lucky for me, a kid runs up to the table and distracts everyone. Being part of Collin's world in this way never really occurred to me. It's been the two of us for so long. Just us as we hide away from Cal and the rest of the world for one reason or another. I almost miss that. I miss having him to myself and not having to share. I could care less if he shares me with anyone, shows me off. I'm much more selfish about my time with him.

Now that we are dating and it's not a secret, selfishness will have to be a thing of the past. He has too many people who care for him. Who need him around. Those people want to drag me into their world too and I don't know if I want it. Can I have Collin without hockey sucking me in as well? It does enough to Collin. I don't want it taking me in too.

Before we leave, I've already been asked to come to lunch and if I'd be willing to help with any fundraising the spouses do.

My selfish heart only hears offers from people who want time with me away from Collin. That is the last thing I want to do, especially right now. Not even considering what Collin is going through, but we are finally a couple. Why would I want to give up couple time to spend with these people? If I separate myself from them, will Collin be okay with that or will he want me to integrate myself as he has?

I've never really been the social type. Not the kind that has a ton of friends. Or even more than two close friends. I had one friend in high school and the Kessy twins. In college, I found a best friend and kept Collin. My circle is super small, just the way I like it.

Collin's is huge. Maybe he can keep his circle and I can have mine, neither having to converge or overlap.

A girl can dream, right?

Collin

"THIS IS BULLSHIT," I huff while leaning back in my seat in Trace's office. "All I want to do is play, and that damn sports psychologist makes it seem like I won't ever do it."

"What happened?" he asks, calm as ever.

I had my first session with my other shrink this morning and I've been agitated ever since. "He's stupid, that's what happened." I power on to what's bugging me the most. "He thinks Cal is my problem." Trace's eyebrows shoot up. "Exactly! We're a force on the ice. One of the reasons management loves us is because we play so well together."

"Then why does he think Cal is your problem?" he asks.

"Because Cal is doing better than me this season, and obviously, right now. He thinks I've compared myself to him so much that it's fucking with my confidence and my play. It's bullshit. He goes back and tells the team that and I won't be playing with my brother."

"How important is that to you?"

My fingers curl and dig into my jeans with his question. "He helps me manage my anxiety, so it's important."

"Okay. That's good. What do you think is your actual problem?"

This is the part I don't want to talk about. I know where things started going downhill for me with hockey; it's fucking embarrassing. Cal would never make such a mistake. Only the dumbass twin would.

"Collin?" Trace urges.

"I scored on Savage, my own goalie. And then I kept fucking up and the pressure not to kept building, but that just made it worse."

He's quiet for far longer than I'd prefer, and when he speaks again, his question surprises me. "Do you trust yourself to handle your anxiety on your own? Without Julie or Cal?"

"We're supposed to have a support system, aren't we?" I ask with confusion, and to also avoid answering his question.

"As long as we don't use it as a crutch. For some people, support systems can be like medication and they rely on them too much. The support system won't always be there. Or be there in the exact moment when you need them. We have to learn how to handle tough situations on our own for those days when we have no other choice."

"I'll never be on my own, though," I point out. "I'll always have Cal."

Trace nods and decides to change the subject, not that I mind. "How are things with Julie?"

"Good. She has a job now. So I get to stay at the house with a stupid cat by myself." I would never say so, but I'd hate life even more if it wasn't for Marmalade. I never realized how much he keeps me company until I was without Julie and hockey during the day.

"And your anxiety?"

I shrug. "I'm antsy feeling all the time." I share that I've started running with Brayden again, because he threatened me if I didn't, and the pathetic practicing I do get. The team is about to go on a road trip. The first one I won't be on. I've never been so jealous of Cal as I am right now. The only thing holding me together is the fact that I keep reminding myself I can spend that time with Julie and Julie alone. But it'll still suck because she's found her a job, so my days will be spent with Marmalade. "I've become a whiner," I blurt out. "Nothing is good enough, satisfying enough, because I'm not playing. I should be on top of the world right now because I'm finally in a relationship with Julie, but I keep finding shit to bitch about because it's not enough."

When did I become an ungrateful asshole?

Without waiting to see what Trace will say, I stand. "I'm done for today." This is the last place I want to be and he's not the person I want to discuss this with. Julie is who I need. Not that I can speak with her right now; she's working.

With the limited bright side I can see, I am glad Jules

has a job. She's been happier since she's had something to look forward to every day. We all like to have a purpose. She has hers with her job. Plus, she's trying to *fix* me. And I say that in the nicest way possible. She doesn't ask me about my day when she gets home because she knows I'll only gripe. She helps with whatever is left to do with dinner while telling me about her day. Not once does she mention hockey. She has gotten it in her head that it plays too big a role in my life. As if that's possible.

She will even get up and leave the room if Cal's and my conversation lasts too long for her taste. It actually bothers me a bit. She's always been supportive until now. At least, it kind of feels that way. She was invited out with the women; I've never seen her reject someone so fast. Maybe it's because of how things went at the last get-together.

My mind swirls, obsessing over how to make my two worlds come together cohesively, until Julie gets home. Marmalade stands on my lap. His tail sways and he watches her drop her things on the table by the door, toe out of her shoes, and walk over to me.

"You haven't started dinner? Shame on you," she tsks with a smile. Julie sits next to me and Marmalade saunters to her lap, already purring.

"Why didn't you want to go out with the women when they asked you?"

Julie looks at me, her smile gone. "What?"

"You heard me," I gently reply. "Is it because of what happened at the party?"

She angles toward me. "Collin, we've known each other a long time. During that time, you can count on one hand the number of friends I've had. My circle is small, always has been. Your circle is *huge*. I don't know what to do with that."

Oh. Well, that makes sense. She was likely over-whelmed. Julie isn't the kind of social person who has a ton of friends; I consider myself the same way, but it's different with hockey and with the team. It just is.

"You're not mad, are you?" she asks.

"No. I wanted to understand why. Maybe you can make friends with at least one of them, then? You should have someone else here besides me and your new co-workers, Jules."

She stares at me for a minute before nodding. "I can try."

I smile, happy to hear it. "Sydney or Raelynn or Deanna would be your best bets. I'd try Deanna first."

Julie laughs. "Help me remember who they are, Collin. Of course I know Deanna."

"Sydney was the one who you met while you were on the porch at the party; Raelynn dates EJ. She used to be his nanny."

The only one I can't really match the name to her face is Raelynn. "Set me up on a playdate with whomever you'd like, Collin."

I grin. "Thank you." I give her a quick kiss. "And I know I've moped around lately; I don't want to do that anymore."

"You're going through a tough time; it's understand-able."

"I know, but I could handle it a little better." I rest my forehead against hers. "You going to keep me in check?"

"Haven't I always?"

123

With the team on an away trip, my anxiety takes another nosedive. My phone stays glued to my hand. Articles about the team are almost always up and ready for me to devour. The team has gained some stride; doing well right now. Is that because I'm not with them? Was I what was causing our team to fail? Thinking like this isn't doing me any good, I know, but there is nothing else for me to do.

This doesn't even touch on the few writers who still talk about me. Where am I? How long will I be out exactly? A new fire has been lit because I was spotted on the ice two days ago by someone. All I wanted to do was get some ice time in. Someone had to ruin it by saying that there appeared to be nothing wrong with me at all, which brings into question whether the team is being honest with the media. It's a bunch of bullshit.

We do share one question in common, though: when will Collin Kessy be back on the ice? I ask my stupid sports psychologist at our next session. His answer pisses me off. "When you're ready."

"I'm ready now," I tell him.

He shakes his head and asks me once again how I feel about having hardships with hockey when Cal isn't having any trouble. I might be the one with problems, but he's the psycho. He tells me flat-out that he thinks I compare myself to Cal too much. We're twins. We're the same. What's to compare?

"Another bad day?" Julie asks when she gets home from work later that day.

"Yeah. Now he thinks I compare myself to Cal way

too much."

Julie averts her gaze and showers Marmalade with a tad too much attention. I still wait for her response, but it quickly becomes apparent I won't get one. "You think that too? Why?" I ask, my voice swirling with hurt and confusion.

Her eyes cut to mine in a heartbeat. "I don't know if compare is the right word for it." Julie sighs and drags her feet as she decides to come sit next to me. "You put him on a pedestal." She makes a face of disgust. "Cal is the one without any problems," she begins in a mocking tone. "Cal is the good one. Cal is the better one. Why can't I be like Cal? We're supposed to be identical, so why aren't we?" She fakes a gag. "You think he's better than you and you're always trying to catch up; you think you can't live your life without him. That's a crock of bullshit, Collin, and you'd know that if you'd open your eyes."

Before I can get a word in, she continues, full of a fire I didn't know she had in her. "What about when you retire, Collin? Am I supposed to live in the same town as Cal for the rest of my life? What if Cal meets a woman who wants to live in another state than you? Will you guilt trip him into staying nearby? You're twins and you have a special bond; I understand that, but you are two separate people and at some point, you have to stop wondering why you have a harder life than Cal. Maybe it's because the powers that be knew you could handle it and he can't."

I don't know what to focus on first, but I find something to say anyway. "You think I handle my anxiety?"

She grabs my hand and squeezes it. "Yes, Collin. And trust me, as frustrated as Cal gets with you, there's no way he could do it." Julie takes a deep breath. "Look, I know you two are great on the ice, but you are great by yourself too." A crooked smile lifts her lips. "Maybe not right now because you're having a hard time, but aside from that, absolutely." Believe it or not, I laugh. "I know you don't like him, but the shrink is right. You compare yourself to your brother too much."

My two weeks is almost up, but it doesn't appear as if I'll be back on the ice any time soon. My head has more issues than I thought.

There's a knock on the door. Julie hops up to answer it. A person on the other side hands her a package, which is odd because it's late to be delivering, but they must have been running late. Then I notice Julie is frozen in the doorway. Her head is bowed, eyes on the package.

"Julie?"

She jumps a mile high and drops the package.

"What's the matter with you?" I ask, standing and picking up the box for her since all she can do is stare at it.

"Nothing. Sorry." She snatches the delivery. "It's just from my parents. I need some privacy to open it." And then she runs into my bedroom and slams the door behind her.

Well, that wasn't weird at all.

Julie

NO. NO, NO, no, no. This can**not** be happening! How did he find me? And so quickly! This is disastrous. I left Florida because of this crazy asshole and now he's come to North Carolina for me. The box sits in my lap, taunting me with what is likely a sickening item that is supposed to be a gift. This is going to ruin everything.

Do I open the box? What good will come from it? Can I even stay in North Carolina now? Should I tell Collin the truth about what really happened? Now is obviously not the best time to tell him that I left home because I was trying to escape a stalker. He got his hands on me once, I shudder at the memory, and I don't need that to happen again.

The timing sucks for me to tell Collin. Not to mention the fact that I've already lied to him. More than once, too, because I didn't tell him about the issue in the first place. I've been lying to him for a year. That will not go over well.

In the end, I decide to stuff the box in the closet. I don't need to know what's in it. Plus, I'm supposed to have dinner with Deanna tonight. Collin did actually set me up on a playdate. Good heavens. What if we go out in public? I'll have to constantly look over my shoulder for *him*. Dwight. Thinking his name causes me to shiver. I don't know what I did to deserve this. To have some horror story come to life like it's right out of a *Criminal Minds* episode.

Only I'm not dead.

Yet.

The light knock on the bedroom door startles me so much I gasp and my heart races. "Jules? Deanna is here."

With a deep steadying breath, I open the door and force a smile. "Great. Are you sure you don't want to come with us?" I ask, though it's a bad idea knowing Dwight is out there.

"I'll be fine here."

He nudges me to where Deanna awaits with a smile. We exchange hellos and then are on our way. My gaze flits to every crook and nanny as if Dwight might stuff his body there, waiting to jump out and grab me.

"Is everything okay, Julie?" Deanna asks once we get into her car. "You seem tense. You don't have to go if you don't want to. Collin just said he wanted you to make friends and I had a leg up." She laughs a little as she backs out of her parking space.

"I'm fine. Sorry; there's a lot on my mind."

"How is he doing, if you don't mind me asking?"

"He's making progress. I think he'll need to be back on the ice soon for him to truly feel better."

She nods as if she understands. "Brayden had a concussion not too long ago." Deanna shakes her head. "He was such a grump. It's like they lose part of themselves when they can't play. It's harder for Brayden because the r-word comes around him every so often."

"The r-word?" I ask with confusion.

"Retirement," she explains. "At one point, he couldn't even see himself retiring." Deanna shrugs. "He's realizing it'll happen, though."

At least I know this is normal for Collin. I ask Deanna about her business, catch up with that, and by that time, we've arrived at a restaurant.

"I hope you don't mind, but I invited Sydney. I thought about inviting Raelynn, I like her, but you seemed to like Sydney a little more. Plus, she can get a babysitter a little easier than Raelynn."

"That's fine."

Sydney sits at the table already. I like the place they've chosen. It's a casual restaurant that serves Southern comfort food, exactly what I need tonight. We spend the first few minutes deciding what to eat and placing our orders. All I can think about is Dwight and whether I should tell Collin.

It's no surprise that I blurt out, "Do you keep secrets from your boyfriends? Husband?" I correct when looking at Sydney.

Their eyes widen. Sydney is the first to speak.

"Tell him. Don't keep a secret. Granted, my secret was huge and I did sort of try to tell Ian, but I could have tried harder. Tell him. It's not worth what it will do to your relationship, Julie."

Deanna nods her head. "If it's the real thing, don't wait to talk and don't keep anything from him. I did it one time with Brayden and it will be the last time. His anger and hurt wasn't worth it."

"How long did you keep the secret?" I ask.

"Years," Sydney answers first and then Deanna says, "Maybe a few weeks, if that?"

"Do you want to talk about it?" Sydney asks.

"No." Deanna's hand lands on mine. "You can't tell us and not tell Collin. That won't go over well either. Unless you plan to tell him, too?" Then her eyes narrow. "Does this have anything to do with those bruises you had?"

"What bruises?" Sydney asks.

The bell jingles loudly over the noise of the restaurant and draws my attention to the door.

There he is.

Dwight.

He smiles at me and takes a seat at an empty table.

"Julie?"

I force myself to focus on the company I'm with. "What if he can't help me? What if no one can help me?" Dwight has been successfully eluding the police in Florida for months and the police here don't even know about my situation.

The women exchange a look. "Julie, what is going on?" Deanna asks.

"You know what, forget it. I'll tell Collin," I lie. I ask Sydney about her kids and her husband and at least get the conversation on a different topic, although it takes a moment before they go with it.

Our food comes a little bit later. Before we dive in, Sydney needs a restroom break and Deanna says she does too.

No.

If I go with them, I have to walk past Dwight.

If I don't, I'm left alone.

There is no good option here.

Being near him is as dangerous as staying put. Crowded restaurant and friends near or not, if he wants me to come with him, he will find a way to do it and threaten me in just the right way so I'll cooperate.

Trust me, I know.

In the end, I decide to stay. Maybe he will watch from a distance. I can't help but watch him. Wait to see what his next move will be. The moment the women walk past him, he stands and heads my way. A cinder block settles in my stomach. If I get up and make a run for it, he'll only follow.

Dwight takes Deanna's seat.

"That was sneaky of you, Julie. Booking a flight to New York, but getting off at one of your layovers and driving to another airport. It took me longer than I'd like to admit to figure out why you weren't in the Big Apple. But now, I've found my angel." He grins and puke rises in my throat. "Did you like your gift?"

"I haven't opened it."

Dwight frowns. "Well, open it when you get home." His frown deepens. "Speaking of, you need to come back with me. Living with that guy is unacceptable." He manages a shrug. "But we'll fix that soon enough. I do like that you're allowing me to play my favorite game of cat and mouse again." He checks his watch and stands. "Until we meet again, Julie." My body turns to solid ice as he leans over and kisses my cheek. "I'll be watching," he adds in a whisper.

The door to the restaurant swings closed as my new friends are walking out of the bathroom.

What in the world am I supposed to do now?

Dwight is in his torture-by-watching stage right now. Everywhere I go, he makes sure I spot him. Go to the grocery store with Collin? He's holding an apple in the fruit and veggie section as if he's shopping too. Leaving work? He's parked in a space I'll have to walk by to get to my car. Go to a game since Collin is playing again? He does one of those stupid dances to get himself noticed and on the big screen so I'll see him.

The man is everywhere.

This phase won't last long, but I prefer it to the next one. The next one is scarier. Waiting for it is torture. I still haven't told Collin. He's so happy and making progress both on and off the ice. Cal will kill me if I'm the one to ruin that.

Which brings me to something else I've contemplated: telling Cal. It's crazy, I know. But some stupid part of me thinks if I tell him, he can help me keep the secret from Collin while figuring out what to do. Running didn't help.

The police can't manage to catch him. At least those in Florida never could.

I've even thought that maybe I'm not meant to be happy. Otherwise, why would I have so much bad luck? What if I've done something at some point for me to deserve what Dwight wants from me?

"Jules." A kiss lands on my temple and it's followed by a sigh. "Talk to me," Collin pleads. "Why aren't you happy?"

"I'm happy," I protest, but I can't get the truth to convey fully in my voice.

He shakes his head. "Something has changed; you don't act the same. Let me fix it."

This is it. The perfect opportunity to tell him.

Cal bursts through the door. "We're in!"

"What?" Collin asks, his mind still on me.

"Boston lost. We're going to the playoffs."

I've never understood exactly how a team gets into the playoffs when it comes down to the final hour, but apparently, the Carolina Rebels are going. I don't even know how we got to April as fast as we did.

But I know I lost my perfect opportunity thanks to Cal.

Cal walks straight to the fridge and grabs three beers. He hands one to each of us. "Let the journey be tough but let us be tougher." He clinks the neck of his beer against ours and takes a seat next to his brother. "What do you think our chances are?"

"Well, we're the underdog and barely squeaked in," Collin says, giving me an uneasy look. He much prefers we still be having a private conversation.

Cal rolls his eyes. "Have more faith."

He's talking to Collin, but I feel as if he's talking to me. I need to have more faith. In myself, in Collin, in the police. The first thing I need to do is take my copy of police reports, the gifts Dwight has sent, and see what the police here may be able to do. And then, I need to tell Collin.

I rest my head on Collin's shoulder while the twins talk. This entire situation is wearing me down.

"You okay, Julie?" Cal asks.

"That's it! Even Cal can tell something is wrong," Collin exclaims, his eyes wide with worry.

"I'm fine," I reassure them both. "I'm tired is all." I kiss Collin's cheek and then stand. "I should get some rest. Good night, guys." Before Collin can argue with me, I hurry to our bedroom. I've been so emotionally and mentally exhausted that I've had no trouble falling asleep lately. Today is no different.

Collin

JUST WHEN MY life is getting back on track, something else is falling apart. Once I agreed with my sports psycho, it took one week before I was cleared to practice again with the team. Granted, I have had to really analyze my relationship with my brother. They *may* have been right about a few things. I'm working on it. That and keeping my anxiety under control. The new meds are helping a lot, but I'm still having some day-to-day anxiety as well as some where hockey is concerned.

Playing in that game last night did wonders for my soul. I felt like myself for the first time in ages. It took until the third period to fully shake my nerves, but I don't mind. Things will only continue to get better.

The next step is to become fully confident again and figure out what the hell is going on with my girlfriend. She's been acting unusual for weeks now. What I don't understand is why she isn't confiding in me. We've always been able to talk to one another, but she's holding back.

"She's not talking to you?" Cal asks, reminding me that he's still here.

"No. She says she's fine, but…" my voice trails off.

"She's lying," Cal confirms.

I glance over at him. "You see it too?" When he nods, I frown. "I don't know why she won't talk to me."

"Who knows when it comes to Julie." Believe it or not, Cal has been a lot nicer toward Julie. They've reached a point where they can get along without snapping at one another. It's made my life a lot easier and everyone a lot happier.

My gaze moves to my closed bedroom door. Life doesn't want anyone to be completely happy all the time, though. Otherwise, I wouldn't be sitting here, worried about Julie. Things get better, things get worse. Never are all things all better at once. But I made a promise to myself to be more positive. Julie is here. I am back with the team and not playing terribly. Cal and Julie are getting along. All of that counts for something.

Cal hangs around for a while before leaving me alone. I eventually join a sleeping Julie. Even asleep, she looks unhappy. Her lips dip downward the tiniest bit. There's a wrinkle between her brows. Her eyes seem to be squeezed so tightly closed as if there's something in our world running after her and she's closing her eyes before the terrible blow.

I draw her into my arms, hoping for a tomorrow where Julie doesn't have any worries on her mind.

In the morning, I find Julie snuggled so close against me. Her nails dig into my side with enough bite to be uncomfortable. But the cutest little snore rattles up from the back of her throat and makes me smile. Something is bothering my Jules; I will be getting to the bottom of it. It's confirmed when I lightly run my hand down her back and it startles her awake.

Her eyes don't flash open with pleasant surprise, but straight up terror.

"Jules," I whisper. "I didn't mean to scare you." That has never scared her before.

She blinks for a solid thirty seconds, as if she isn't quite there and it takes that long for her to come to her senses. "Hi."

"Hey."

"I had a nightmare, I think," she explains.

"Do you want to talk about it?"

"I don't really remember it." She hides her face in the crook of my neck.

"Want to talk about what's been bothering you then?"

"Collin," she whispers.

"Julie," I whisper back.

She giggles. "I love you."

"I love you too. I'd love you more if you'd trust me and tell me what is going on."

Julie sighs. "I need some time. I do trust you, too."

But she's scared; that much is evident. I don't know how else to soothe her fear, whatever that might be exactly. She's closing me out, but she also isn't budging. For now, I'll let it go.

For now.

I grab her wrists and quickly move us so Julie lies on her back with me on top of her. There's a subtle, immediate change when she gets horny. Her breathing shallows out for one quick second. I grin and grind my hips against hers.

"Excited, Jules?"

"About what?" she asks plainly, causing my grin to widen.

"If you don't want me, I can go take my shower." I pull myself away only an inch's worth and Julie tugs me back.

"I do want you, Collin."

That's all I need to hear, so I lean down to kiss her.

"Nervous?" Cal asks just loud enough for me to hear him as we skate on the ice during warm ups. "Because of Julie, I mean."

It's game night and Julie is here watching. It took way more convincing than I thought it would to get her to come to a game, but she relented eventually.

Am I nervous?

"No," I answer honestly. "She didn't want to come," I admit.

"Because of the spouses?" he questions.

For some reason, I don't think that was it, but I simply shrug.

"Well, let's focus on what's important right now: the game."

Despite what I told my twin, there is some anxiety spreading through my veins. I don't think it's because Julie is here watching me, though. There is no time to dwell on it; the puck drops before I feel ready mentally. One of the things I've learned is how to effectively shut down my incessant thoughts and find one purpose. My purpose right now is to regain puck control.

I'm within reach of the guy in front of me. My stick stretches out ahead of me, to his right. If I could just graze the puck enough to slip it from his grasp. Cal comes up on my side, momentarily distracting him just long enough for me to close more of the space between us, and swipe the puck. In one swift move, I turn and send the puck to the nearest Rebel, who can take off and face the goalie. His shot is fast and good.

Celebrating with my teammates feels surreal compared to where I was a few weeks ago. But I'll savor every second on the ice because I don't know when I'll have my last shift. It could be years from now, or it could be tonight if some unfortunate injury were to happen. But my anxiety won't get in the way again if I can help it.

The game wears on, becoming more and more physical. I won't have to worry about my anxiety wearing me out tonight; the game is doing that for me. This game gets intense too. Three fights break out in the third period, energizing the crowd to a height not yet reached tonight. My head stays up. My nerves stay level. And I make it through without any major issues. I'd call that a successful night.

Cal

I'M ALMOST TO my apartment door when a pair of footsteps from behind me causes me to glance over my shoulder. It's just some guy, but he's watching me with a little too much interest. Enough so that with one hand on my doorknob, I feel compelled to speak to him.

"Can I help you?" I ask. All I want is to fall into bed after the grueling game we had.

"Julie isn't yours to have, you know."

All I can do is stare, dumbfounded. Then it hits me. This guy thinks I'm Collin. "What?" is my genius response. "Who are you?" I tack on.

His head cocks to the side in such a calculating manner, it's unnerving. "Dwight. Julie's fiancé."

My hand falls from the doorknob as I turn to face the guy. "What?" I repeat, partly outraged, partly confused. This is fucking crazy. Julie is a bitch and everything, but surely, she wouldn't do this to my brother.

"See, we got into a fight before she decided to run away and come up here. She obviously didn't tell you about me, but she's come to her senses now. She'll be coming back home with me. I just thought I'd give you a heads-up."

"Why should I believe anything you say?" After all, he's some random guy who followed me into my apartment building to confront me about this shit.

He reaches into his pocket, takes a step forward, and hands me a well-worn folded piece of paper. I open it up to see a photo of the two of them. It has a timestamp with a date soon before I found out about Julie being here. That's all I need to see to have my blood boiling. When I look up, Dwight is gone.

Without any thought, I take two steps to my brother's apartment and bang on the door.

17

Julie

"Y OU!" CAL POINTS an accusatory finger at me. "What the fuck do you think you're doing?"

"Hey!" Collin shoves him back, even though Cal doesn't stand but a few feet inside of the apartment. "What the fuck is your problem?"

I stand as Cal throws a photo my way. "Tell him," he demands as I walk over to pick it up. My heart shatters when I see it. The photo Dwight made me pose for the last time he had me. "Tell him!" Cal shouts again.

"Where did you get this?"

"Your little fiancé caught me outside, thinking I was

Collin," he spits, venom in his voice.

"Fiancé?" Collin asks with confusion.

"Apparently, she's seeing you on the side," Cal tells him.

All I can do is stare at the shaking photo, knowing that Dwight was just outside. He's escalating. He's done waiting. He's coming for me.

It's not until Collin speaks that I realize he's standing in front of me, looking down at the photo as well. "Jules?" My mouth opens to tell him the truth, but the words get hung in my throat. "Is this what you didn't want to tell me?"

"You're such a fucking bitch!" Cal yells, pacing behind his twin as if he's just as affected. Some part of my brain is completely amazed by how Cal is frantic and angry, while Collin is calm and disappointed.

"How do you explain this?" Collin asks, probing me to speak.

"It's not what it looks like," I quietly say, which turns out to be the worst thing to say. Collin's shoulders sag as if I confirmed what Cal told him.

"Get out." Cal comes to stand next to his brother, his voice even and deadly. "If that's all you can say, get the fuck out."

My eyes search Collin's, looking for something contrary to what Cal has said, but I don't see it. "There's an explanation for this." I wave the photo.

"Look at the date," Cal instructs.

I don't need to, but his brother does. And that makes his eyes flash. "This is the bastard that beat you?"

"What?" All the fight leaves Cal.

"You're engaged to him?"

I quickly shake my head. "Never."

"Then what is going on?"

"This doesn't make sense," Cal interjects. "He says she's going back to him, Collin. That this was a break for them after a fight. That she's come to her senses."

"Jules." The pleading in Collin's voice says it all, but still, he says, "You gotta say something."

"It's complicated."

"Try me," he replies instantly.

"He's an ex-boyfriend who won't leave me alone." That's the simplest way to explain it.

Collin isn't happy with that either. His brows furrow as he frowns. "You haven't mentioned dating anyone for," he pauses, doing the math, "almost three years." Yep. And one of those years has been full of living in this hell. When I nod, he shakes his head. "That doesn't make sense," he repeats what his brother has already stated. "He's been chasing you and you didn't tell me? Why would he say you're engaged if you aren't? Why would you take this photo?" He snatches it out of my hand and holds it to my face. "Why would you do this if something wasn't going on? You're fucking smiling in the picture, Julie."

Not a real smile. But it's in that moment of hesitation that Collin's faith in me slips a step too far.

"Maybe it's best if you did leave for the night; I don't need this shit right now when we're in the middle of the playoffs."

And that is when Collin does what he has never done before; he chooses hockey over me.

He's right, though. Now is not the time to explain. We can be saved later. I need to deal with Dwight one way or another. With a curt nod, I grab my purse and walk out the door, expecting to be nabbed at any second.

He's watching; I know he is. The hairs on my arms and the back of my neck are standing tall from the eerie sensation. Once in my car, I call Deanna, asking if I can stay the night. She doesn't let me down, and for that, I'm thankful. It's my last night of peace, I'm sure, before Dwight makes my life hell.

I stand in front of Deanna's door for the longest time, debating if I should knock or turn around and return to Collin.

"Oh, you make this too easy, angel."

I don't get the chance to scream before everything goes black.

Collin

MY EYES RETURN to that picture, over and over again. The more I look at it, the more it looks staged and the more Julie looks like she's forcing herself to look happy. With a sigh, I eventually make my way to my room to stand in front of my closet. If I can distract myself, maybe this will turn out to be a dream instead of a mystery.

I stand there and stare for the longest time. At some point, I begin to rearrange things because our closet is a fucking mess and this gives me something to do, something to focus on.

What is this box? I thought Julie opened this. Wasn't

it a gift from her parents or something? One second I'm about to put it in its new place and the next I'm ripping the box open. The blood drains from my face. There is picture on top of picture on top of yet another picture. All of Julie. What the fuck?

Then I have a terrifying thought.

What is else Julie keeping from me in my own closet?

I tear the closet apart and come across another box. This one has folders inside. And what I find terrifies me.

This is what Julie was trying to say, but couldn't for some reason.

It's police report after police report about a Dwight Travis breaking a restraining order numerous times, and then there are the reports about the abuse. Oh, god. My Jules. Why couldn't you tell me this?

After about the tenth report, I scramble to my feet. Julie left this apartment with a fucking lunatic after her!

And I made her go.

I slip on my shoes, still in sweats and a T-shirt from earlier, and soon cross the hall to bang on my brother's door. He needs to help me not lose my shit while I try to find Julie.

"What?" he answers with a snap a minute later.

"We need to find Julie."

"Why?" he asks, a little more alert now.

"Get dressed and I'll explain."

And I do. Cal may not like Julie all that much, but no one can miss the concern on his face by the time I finish telling and showing him what I found.

"Did she say where she was going?"

"No. I figured we could check Brayden's since she's friends with Deanna before we start hunting down hotels."

And that's when my phone rings with a call from Deanna.

"Hey," I answer. "Is Julie with you? Is she okay?"

"She's not with you? She said she needed a place to crash because you two got into it over her secret, but she never showed."

Oh fuck.

"What, Brayden?" There's a pause and then, as if she's scared to say the words, "Brayden says her car is parked in the driveway. Otis did bark a little bit ago; maybe that was her. But where is she?" I don't get a chance to speak before Deanna says with fear, "Collin, I think something has happened to Julie. Brayden just found her purse on the front porch."

"Call the police and tell them she's been abducted; I'm on my way." I hang up without another word.

"We'll find her," Cal says.

We better. Whatever happens to her will be my fault. I did the one thing I was never supposed to do: I didn't take the time to get to the bottom of what was going on. Instead, I fucking asked her to leave. I'm the reason she's in danger. What the fuck was wrong with me? For years, I've waited for Julie and this part of our life to begin, yet I didn't even fight when she needed me the most. When I get her back, there is a ton of begging for forgiveness I have to do.

"It's not your fault," Cal says, reading my mind.

"All that matters is finding Julie."

By the time we pull into Brayden's driveway, police have already arrived. Talking to them and showing them what I found at home is excruciating. They eventually send us home, concluding that it is very likely Julie was indeed taken.

Sleep isn't an option.

Focus isn't one either, especially when I get an update that one reason why Dwight wasn't in jail is because he's successfully evaded the police in Florida for the past year. Hearing that doesn't bring hope that Julie will be found in a timely manner either. If at all. But I can't think like that because it's not going to help anything.

I thought I felt helpless in the darkest moments of despair when dealing with the worst of my anxiety. That is a drop of water compared to the ocean of helplessness I feel right now. How could I do this to her? How could I do this to us? One decision and everything could be ruined. Julie might not even come back to me.

God, I can't think like that. She will be fine. She will come home.

But the day passes with me sitting at home.

And the night passes without much sleep.

Then while my girlfriend is missing, I have to attend practice. This is the very last place I want to be. Cal was adamant that I tell the team what's going on with Julie, but I've refused. Brayden knows and that's good enough for me. If I can't help Julie, then I need to do what I can to help my team. I don't even know if I can play well enough to do such a thing, but I will definitely try.

Is Julie going to hate me for doing my job while she could be enduring hell?

"Collin."

I look up to see an empty room, except for Brayden and me.

"You don't have to be here," he says.

"Where else am I supposed to be?"

The silence that lingers says enough.

"Look, if you're going to stay, then get your head on straight. Otherwise, you're only going to fuck up and you don't need that on your shoulders either. Let's go." He turns and walks out without waiting to see if I'll follow.

And I do follow because what else am I supposed to do? Sitting here won't help Julie just like sitting at home won't help her. Might as well help my team.

Like old times, when my skate touches the ice, the world disappears. I shut everything down except for the here and now and what's before me. The most important thing right now is doing drills and practicing plays. My thoughts are reduced to simple sentences involving what actions I need to take next.

My perfect, no-problem world crashes the minute we're done and I see a missed call from the police department. There's a voicemail, so I listen to that first. Two minutes later and I discover what a pointless call that was. They don't have a trace of where Julie might be and it sounds like they are discouraged further after speaking more with the detective in charge of Julie's case back in Florida.

As if there's a chance she'll answer, I call Julie.

It rings.

And rings.

And rings.

And then goes to her voicemail.

"Jules," I whisper. "I'm so sorry. We'll get you home. I don't know how yet, but we'll get you home. I love you." With nothing else to say, I hang up.

Needing someone to talk to, I text Trace and ask if I can come in, throwing in that it's urgent. By the time I'm ready to leave the facility, there's a message that I can come as soon as I can. Something is urging me to talk to him and now is not the time for me to get fucked up in the head. Julie needs me too much.

I'm in such a mess with my jumbled thoughts and my anxiety rising up to pump through my veins that it's not until I'm standing in front of a surprised receptionist that I realize my mistake. I'm fully recognizable right now. No hat; it's at home. No sunglasses; forgot them in the truck. No hoodie; it's at home too. Holy shit.

I take a seat closest to the door that leads to the back. With a deep breath, I brave a peek around the waiting room. It's pretty full with about seven other people in here. And one is looking me dead in the eyes.

Fuck.

Without any covertness, he takes his phone out and snaps a photo.

Son of a bitch.

"Mr. Grey?"

I stand and follow the lady to Trace's office. His eyes widen the moment he sees me. "I know. I forgot and I've already had my picture taken. We have bigger problems."

If possible, his eyes grow. "Take a seat and talk to me."

"Julie and I sort of fought because some guy claiming he was her fiancé talked to Cal and said as much. I asked her to leave because I figured I need to focus on hockey right now instead of whatever the fuck was going on. Turns out, he's a stalker and now, she's been taken and I don't know what the fuck to do. The police don't act hopeful for finding her because he's been out of their reach for a year."

Trace leans back in his seat, as if he's taking in all that I've told him. "Sit down, Collin. Take a moment to breathe."

I can't, so I don't.

"Okay," he says, conceding. "How long has she been gone?"

"Since last night. I don't know if I should be practicing and playing, but if I don't, I'll be at home, driving myself crazy. Everything feels wrong. I need to figure out how to find her and bring her home before he hurts her worse than the last time he had her."

"What do you mean?"

Right. I explain how I found Julie at the airport and how it's apparent he was responsible for that. But I don't know how Julie got away. Did he let her go? Did she escape? Could she do it again? At what point is he going to start hurting her again? What if they are no longer in North Carolina?

"What am I supposed to do?" I ask.

"I can't tell you how to cope, Collin. You need to figure out what is best going to help you handle it until Julie comes home. If being with the team helps, do that and don't feel guilty about it. If being at home helps, do that and the team will understand. If you need to park yourself at the police department until you get some news, do that. Whatever will keep you strongest until she gets home because she'll need you to be at your best when she gets back."

"Okay."

"Do you want to talk about the photo?"

I glance up in confusion from where I'd been staring at the floor. "What?"

"You said someone took your photo in the waiting room."

"Oh. Right. No. I'll deal with that later."

The only thing that matters right now is Julie.

19

Julie

"JULES. I'M SO sorry. We'll get you home. I don't know how yet, but we'll get you home. I love you."

My eyes squeeze closed at the sound of Collin's tortured voice.

"Isn't that sweet. Lover boy thinks you're going home." Dwight laughs. "He sounds like such a pansy; what were you doing with him, Julie? Really?"

It's not as if I can respond to him; there's duct tape over my mouth.

"We're almost there, angel. Back to where we began."

I've been lying in the backseat of this car since Dwight stuffed me in it. He has my wrists and ankles taped together. He's been driving on and off since last night; we should have gotten to Florida already, but he keeps stopping for no reason and for longer than necessary. My bladder is about to burst because he's yet to allow me to get out.

When we finally stop, my heart breaks to see where we are. No wonder it took longer than it should have. We're in the Keys. Dwight cuts the tape from my ankles and pulls me out of the car.

"Let's go inside, angel. We have much to do and discuss." He leads me inside a shady-looking house. I look around, hoping someone will see me, but there's not a soul around. How is this possible? Where is everyone?

The inside is bare, except for a couch that looks disgusting with stains in various places. I jerk my arm when he leads me there. He raises an eyebrow. I nod toward the hallway and the bathroom I can see from here.

"Oh, forgive me!" He hurries us to the bathroom. Then he proceeds to lower my bottoms so I can do what I need to while he watches over me. Privacy doesn't exist as long as Dwight is around. He did this last time we were together, so I'm not shocked. I also have to go so badly that I don't care what he does. Thankfully, he does cut the tape over my hands so I can take care of myself.

But as soon as I wash my hands, back goes the tape. As soon as I'm on the couch, the same for my ankles. This is the same as last time, too. What's different is when Dwight brings out a long pair of handcuffs. He cuffs one of my ankles and then cuffs the other to a steel table I didn't notice. The table has been bolted to the floor;

Dwight is prepared for any escape I might try to make.

How will anyone find me? Will they think to look in Florida? Despair clutches my heart. Dwight wasn't prepared last time; it was easier to find a way to escape, but it is clear that he has planned for this. What hope do I have now? He's outsmarted the police for a year.

My heart breaks; tears glide down my cheeks.

The truth thins my blood.

This is where I'll die.

"Angel," Dwight tsks as he squats in front of me, wiping my tears away. "What's the matter? Don't you realize I plan to take good care of you? We will be just fine here, I promise. No one can bother us. We met here. We will live here and live happily."

I nod because I know if I don't, he'll get angry and my fight isn't strong enough for that right now.

Dwight smiles. "Good. I'm tired. I'm going to sleep for a bit before dinner. You rest too." He stands and leaves for the bedroom.

I sag into the couch. At least I'll have some time alone for a bit. Unfortunately, that can be bad too. My mind travels to Collin. How is he handling all of this? He didn't sound too good on the phone. Is he upset with me for not being able to explain everything before I left for Deanna's? At least he knows what's going on. At least he knows I'm missing. It sounded like he did. How much he knows about why depends on if he's found any of the police reports in the closet.

God, I hope so. That'll help things. Although, I'm not sure how much, considering I'm not in North Carolina, nor my hometown in Florida. Damn it, no one will ever find me. The chances that I'll see Collin again are pretty slim.

I've been at this with Dwight long enough to know that me escaping will be next to impossible.

Praying isn't something I normally do. However, I find myself closing my eyes and asking the Lord to get me back to North Carolina in one piece and alive.

The second longest week of my life passes with Dwight feeding me, watching TV with me, and increasing the amount of physical contact he has with me. It's been a week and I'm still here. A week of Dwight making me watch Collin play hockey, seemingly unfazed. A week of hearing reporters discuss a photo of him at a therapist's office. It was taken the day after I left.

Collin hasn't commented on it yet, but the team released a statement that they are aware of all the health issues with all of their players. A simple way to say that whatever Collin is going to therapy for is known to the team.

The longer I'm here, the more faith I lose in hoping I'll be found.

The longer I'm here, the more Dwight talks about making love.

And the more he talks about that, the more I think about death.

His or mine. Whichever could come first. Whichever prevents that line from being crossed. Dwight is patient and a sort of tease in this respect, but his patience is waning every day. I constantly look for something I could use to injure him or to aid in an escape, but Dwight is too careful. He learned from his previous mistakes and he's not making them again.

"Why?" I croak, unable to take the unknown any longer. Why did he pick me? How?

Dwight turns his head toward me. "What?"

"Why did you come after me? How did you pick me?"

His slow, evil smile makes me regret asking. "Do you want to know how I came to meet you, angel?" He doesn't give me a chance to speak. He utters an answer that has me horrified. Something that absolutely can't be true. Something I refuse to believe. It just can not be possible. As soon as he says it, I block it from my mind and try to forget he ever said it.

Then, at the beginning of the second week, Dwight has it on the hockey channel and I perk up at hearing Collin's name.

"We would like to take a moment to discuss a serious matter. It has come to our attention that Collin Kessy's girlfriend has gone missing." My eyes bulge at seeing a photo of Collin and me on the screen. "She's been missing for eight days now. Kessy was keeping the matter private, even from his team we hear, but he's decided to reach out to the public in case anyone has spotted Julie Lockwood. It is believed that she's in extreme danger and—"

Dwight turns the TV off. "Who the fuck does he think he is? Doesn't he know that he's not your boyfriend? And you aren't in any danger, Julie! Look at you! Haven't I taken good care of you?" I quickly nod. "I have!" Dwight stands and paces. "What a fucking stupid thing for him to do. You'll be all over the news now." His rage turns into mumblings.

I send up both a thank you that he's trying and curse him because Dwight turns, charges, and unleashes his rage on me.

Dwight hits my jaw. After about the fifth blow, there's a banging on the front door. All I can do is slump over. Thank goodness for the intrusion because my vision is blotchy. I don't know how much more I could take. I struggle to watch Dwight open the door just enough to poke his head out.

"What?" he snaps.

"Is everything okay? I thought I heard yelling."

"I'm fine." He slams the door and faces me.

I close my eyes, hoping he'll think I've blacked out and leave me be.

Please Collin. Find me.

Darkness sweeps into a delirious dream that's much better than my current reality.

"Jules."

I sigh with relief, smile, and run to Collin. "You found me!"

"Of course I did," he replies, wrapping his arms around me. "You're hurt."

"I'm okay," I say. I don't think I'm hurt. I feel fine. "I'm sorry."

"Me too."

"I love you."

"I love you too. Let's get out of here."

Collin takes my hand, but when he walks away, I'm yanked to a stop. I glance down and break into tears at seeing my restraints.

"Don't worry, Julie. I just forgot to free you." He

waves his hand over my ankles, causing the chains to fall and clank to the floor. "Now we can go."

"Where are we going?" I ask as he finally leads me away.

"To where no one can ever find us."

"Just you and me?"

"Just you and me," he confirms.

Outside, the heat of the sun warms my face. I forgot how good that felt. Collin tugs me further until we walk onto the beach. The sand wiggles between my toes as my feet sink into the grains. Oh, I love the sand.

"Are you listening?" Collin asks.

The sound of crashing waves booms suddenly, startling me. My eyes instinctively close as I listen to the water come and go.

"Listen harder, Jules. Listen past the waves."

What am I supposed to hear?

Is it a baby? There's something wailing. No. Screaming.

POP!

As much as I can, I curl into myself. More gunshots fire, but I can't tell from where, except that they are entirely too close. There's yelling, but I can't distinguish anything.

"Clear!"

I jump a foot off the couch when someone gently touches my shoulder.

"Julie?"

With a hesitant look, I fall apart upon seeing the police officer.

"You're okay. I'm going to take this duct tape off,

okay? Paramedics are on the way."

I hold my wrists out and he begins to slowly and painfully remove the tape. He motions to my mouth next and I nod.

"I need you to sit up, sweetie," he says softly.

Oh. With a wince and a whimper, I manage to do so. By the time I'm free of the tape, the paramedics have arrived and they are working on removing the cuffs.

"How did you find me?" I ask the officer, who remains standing nearby with a watchful eye.

"We've been receiving tips of sightings, but nailed a location when a neighbor recognized him from the photo your boyfriend had blasted on the media and called it in."

Collin shared Dwight's photo too? Thank god. He just saved me.

"Can you call him?"

The man, about my dad's age, smiles. "Already done, sweetie. I imagine he's finding a way down here as we speak."

20

Collin

I DESPISE HOW long it took for me to go to the media. Struggling over that decision was stupid, but within hours of Julie's and Dwight's pictures being blasted, I got a call that it seemed Dwight had been sighted in Florida.

Florida.

Julie might not even be in North Carolina. How am I supposed to find her if she's not here? I'm slowly losing my mind. I don't know how much longer I can keep this up; not to mention, there's no telling what is happening to Julie.

We made it through the first round and I don't remember any of the experience. There's a short break before we enter the second round. I'm hoping that's when we'll find Julie. My first day of rest involves a lot of thinking about going to Florida and figuring out how to hunt her down myself. The guilt is eating me alive; I can't take this anymore and I need to find Julie.

But then, I get a phone call.

The man talks and says some things, but all I hear is, "We found her."

"Collin?"

"They found her," I repeat to my brother, who watches me like a hawk.

He takes the phone from me, listens, says thank you, and then hangs up. "Pack a bag; we need to go get her."

"Is she okay?"

Cal pauses for a second and then nods. "She's fine. Go." He nods toward my bedroom. I don't hesitate to grab a few things in case Julie can't come home immediately as Cal seems to think.

Within minutes, we're both back in the living room with a bag each.

"I got us plane tickets; I assume you want the fastest route possible?"

"Yes."

"Let's go then. Our flight leaves in three hours."

The waiting now is almost as bad as the waiting before. Julie is safe now, but what kind of shape is she in? Is she mad at me that I made her leave when she needed me most? That's not important right now. I need to get my eyes on Julie and make sure she's okay.

But first I must wait in the airport and on the plane. Wait during a short layover in Charlotte. Wait for the rental car once in Florida. Wait as Cal drives us to the hospital where Julie is being held. Wait to find out what room she's in. Wait to be let in.

And then I see her.

She's asleep.

Her face is bruised and swollen. There's no telling what else is bruised on her body, too.

But she looks relaxed and at ease.

My brother nudges my back for me to step further into the room. I do. One step after another until I stand next to her bed. Her hand is curled into a fist. There are red lines on her arms around her wrists. Do I want to know why those are there?

Carefully, I take her hand.

Big mistake.

Julie gasps, lurches upright, and looks scared as hell.

"Hey, it's just me. I'm sorry. I'm so sorry; I didn't mean to scare you."

Her wide eyes blink rapidly. The moment reality hits, her shoulders sag, tears fall from her eyes, and she whispers, "Collin." I gently pull her into my arms. Her head rests on my shoulder. I glance over at Cal while she sobs. He shrugs. There's nothing I can say right now. Nothing that will do justice, so I hold her.

Some time passes before she leans back to look at me.

"Are you actually here?"

"Yeah. Are you?" I ask.

"God, I hope so."

I smile.

"How are you feeling?"

Cal's voice startles Julie once again. She looks over at him dumbfounded.

"What are you doing here?" she asks in a genuinely curious manner.

"Because my brother loves you. So, how are you feeling?" he repeats.

"I could be better." Julie glances back at me. "Do you know when I can go home?"

"We just got here, but we'll find out," I promise.

Julie frowns. "Do you know what happened to Dwight?"

I look to Cal, who simply shakes his head. Before either of us can answer, two more people rush into the room. Julie's frown deepens as her parents push Cal and me aside to crowd their daughter. Cal and I step over by the window to give them all space.

"Dwight's dead," he whispers. "There was a shootout or something."

And Julie was in the middle of it? We're lucky she wasn't hurt. I can't stop surveying her body, searching for injuries. And where is a nurse? Or a doctor? Shouldn't they be in here checking her out? Should she even be talking to her parents? There's a lot of talking going on.

"Stop!" Julie suddenly screams, which does cause a nurse to rush in. "Get out! I don't need to deal with this!"

"Okay," the nurse says. "I think Julie needs some peace and quiet. Everyone out."

Neither I nor my brother move, but Julie's parents leave the room. The nurse faces us with a resting bitch face.

"They can stay," Julie tells her before she can try to get us to leave.

"Fine, but you need to rest." The nurse glares at Cal and me, as if we had anything to do with Julie's outburst, and then she leaves.

Julie falls back onto her uprighted bed with a sigh. "I love my parents, but they just don't know how to act sometimes." She frowns and winces. "I forgot to ask when I can leave. If I never come back to Florida again, I'll be just fine." Jules looks over at me. "Is it okay if I sleep?"

I walk over to her bed and take her hand. "Get all the rest you need, Jules. We'll be right here when you wake up."

"Thanks, Collin." Her eyes close and then she peeks them open again. "You too, Cal." Her eyelids fall shut and within seconds she's knocked out.

Collapsing into the nearby chair, I look at my brother.

"She's safe; there's nothing else to worry about," he says.

"I know. Do you want to let everyone know she's with us now?"

Cal nods and steps out of the room. For the first time in what feels like months, I relax. There's still much ahead to be tackled, but the worst is behind us.

Hopefully.

Julie is discharged the next day. All she has talked about is going home, so the airport is our first stop. She's been quiet, but that's expected. After a police officer came by to check on her, gather her statement and informed her of Dwight's death themselves, she's had even less to say. If she's not sleeping, she's attached to my hip, not that I'm complaining at all.

Her head rests upon my shoulder as we fly home, her hand in mine. "How are you doing?" she asks quietly.

"Fine," I reply, a little confused.

"But everyone knows now and you were worried about that."

Oh. Damn. With everything that's happened to her, she was still able to find out how my picture at Trace's office made its round on social media. Someone in either his or Dr. Gressley's office leaked why I was there because Dr. Gressley's name came up and my anxiety issues were blasted.

And now she's asking how I'm doing?

"It doesn't even matter, Jules. The team's PR people have been handling it for me; I don't care. I've been focused on bringing you home."

"That's good." There's a pause and then, "Do I still have my job?"

"Yeah, Jules. Don't worry about that. We'll get home, you can rest, and then you can think about working." Hell, if she wanted to hole up in my apartment for a few weeks, I wouldn't say a thing. She needs to decompress and find a way to put this behind her, to start that process.

I already plan to have Deanna be with her as much as possible since the second round starts tomorrow. Trace said he would be willing to speak with her if she wanted to talk to someone. Julie will get whatever she needs. I've even told the team that if she says she needs me to stay, I plan to stay and miss however many games necessary. I will not put her second again.

"Did y'all make it to the next round?" she asks.

"Yeah. Starts tomorrow." Thank god we get to kick it off at home.

"Oh." A simple, lackluster reply.

"I plan to stay with you as long as you want me to," I reassure her.

She lifts her head. "You can play, Collin. I'll be fine."

"We'll talk about it later."

Her head returns to my shoulder and remains there throughout the rest of the flight. At some point, I realize she's fallen asleep once again.

"What will you do about the games?" Cal asks. "Do you really think she's okay?"

"I don't know and no, I don't."

"No one will blame you for staying out. Everyone knows family comes first."

That's true. While I feel as if both of my families need me right now, there is only one who will make the ultimate decision.

A few hours later, Julie and I walk through my apartment door. Thankfully, Cal takes his leave of us then. It's been nice to have him nearby, but his work is done. Marmalade goes nuts over Julie. He rubs his body against her legs, purring louder than I've ever heard him. It takes Julie all of two seconds to pick him up.

"I've never heard his motor that loud," I comment as I drop my bag in one of the chairs. "He missed you."

"I missed him too."

That much is obvious. Marmalade nuzzles his head against her face and she's smiling wider than I've seen since I arrived at the hospital. I've talked plenty of shit about Marmalade, but never again. This moment right here, watching something as simple as a damn cat make her happy after she just survived hell? Marmalade is officially my cat.

"Come sit, Jules," I say as I take a seat on the couch. She comes over and sits next to me, curling into my side with Marmalade on her lap. "Anything you want to do for the rest of the evening?"

"No. Maybe take a bath, but otherwise, I don't want to do anything at all."

That will be easy to accomplish.

She looks up at me. "I want you to play, Collin. Let's get back to normal; that's normal."

"Are you sure? The team will be fine without me." She nods her head twice. "Okay. If that's what you want. Trace said you can talk to him if you want, too. You can obviously talk to me if you want, but I didn't know if you might want to talk to someone else."

"This isn't the first time I've been through this, Collin," she says plainly. "I'll be fine. I just need a few weeks to readjust and let it hit me that he's really gone."

All I can do right now is keep an eye on her and take her word for it.

Julie

I ACHE.

    I hurt.

    I'm still exhausted.

Collin invites me to his game tonight, but I turn him down. Only because I don't want to face those women when I look so beat up. Maybe they will respect my privacy, but even if they do, my body just hurts too much to get out and about.

I did call work to let them know I'm back in town. I'll return next week. They have no idea how grateful I am that they are working with me. They told me to take the rest of the week off; I didn't even have to ask. That wouldn't have happened back home. I know because it happened the last time Dwight took me.

Collin has been gone most of the day. It's been surprisingly nice to be here alone with Marmalade to keep me company. Collin's worry is evident, though. There are sticky notes in various places around the apartment with his therapist's number on it. He also wrote a little note to call Deanna if I want. What he failed to mention, that I learn when there is a knock on the door, is that Deanna is coming over to watch the game with me.

"Should I go?" Deanna asks when I open the door. "You don't look happy to see me. I brought wine." She shakes the bottle of wine in her hand.

"I didn't know you were coming." I step aside for her to come in. "But you have wine." Hopefully my smile looks real. "Shouldn't you be at the game, though?" I ask as she makes her way to the kitchen.

"Brayden is so focused on hockey right now, he won't miss me not being there. Besides, a little birdie told me that he would be able to relax if he knew you had company, so here I am." All the while she's talking, she's rummaging through the kitchen to search for a corkscrew. "Grab some glasses and help me out, will you?"

I do as she asks and give her the corkscrew as well.

"Have you had dinner yet?" she asks and I shake my head, causing her to sigh. "Julie, you're killing me." She pours us each a glass of wine before placing an order for Chinese food. "Let's sit."

Since my evening is officially in the hands of someone else, I follow her lead. I wait for her to ask me the inevitable "how are you" question. It makes me realize how anxious I am over being asked such a simple question, too.

Instead, Deanna talks gossip. I don't even know some of the people she's talking about. But I'm grateful for what she's doing because it allows me to slowly relax.

Our food is delivered just as the game starts.

Four minutes in, Collin scores a goal. Maybe I'm crazy, but his celebration seems different.

"He was in bad shape while you were..." Deanna's voice trails off. "Gone," she finishes. "It may not have shown on the ice, but he was in therapy or on the phone with his therapist every day. Cal and Brayden wouldn't leave him alone either. He has a lot of guilt about what happened before..."

Before? It takes me a minute to realize exactly what she's talking about. "Him asking me to leave, you mean?" Deanna nods in confirmation. "That doesn't really matter, though." Dwight would have gotten to me one way or another. "He shouldn't feel guilty."

"Maybe you should tell him that."

We fall silent as an underwear commercial comes on.

"Are you okay?" Deanna finally asks.

"Yeah."

"Think we'll win?"

I smile. "I hope so. We could all use more wins." It's then and there that I decide to take full advantage of this game and Deanna as a distraction. I turn toward her a bit. "Can I ask you something?"

"Sure."

"Do you like being immersed into their world? Being around all the spouses and other players? Being involved in the community they have going?"

Deanna seems to mull over my question before answering. "I'm only involved as much as I want to be, but yes, I enjoy it. I…I don't have much family and it was like I gained a great big family. There are ups and downs, but one thing remains true: the Rebels are *always* there for one another." She seems to let me think about this before she asks, "Why do you ask?"

"I don't know if you've noticed, but I tend to stick to myself. The Rebels family is intimidating and overwhelming. I was kind of hoping I could just stick with Collin." Her eyes widen a little. "And you and Brayden." As an afterthought, I add, "And Cal."

Deanna laughs. "Believe it or not, there are little cliques within the spouses. We could be your clique. And nothing is expected. If it is, then," she shrugs, "oh well. You do what you want. Have you told Collin?"

"With all that's going on, I can't even remember if I have or not."

"Don't worry about things like this, Julie. Really. Do what you want and it'll all work out. Something tells me Collin doesn't care how involved or uninvolved you are."

The blaring of a horn drags our attention back to the TV; the Rebels have scored again. I let our talk fall to the wayside and focus on the game. For the first time in two weeks, in months, I feel decent. Good, even.

We watch the extremely physical game; I'd forgotten how brutal a playoff game can be. From the hits to the fights to the aggressive play, teams transform their behavior and push everyone to their limits. I'm not much of a fan, at least I don't consider myself one, but I can get lost in a game. Watching players rush down the ice, swiveling around another player, standing idly at times during a power play and trying to decide what to do. It's all fascinating.

Deanna keeps a steady pour on our wine glasses to keep them full until the bottle is empty. I curl up on the couch, leaning on the throw pillow.

The game gives way to a dark room with Dwight rambling nonsense as he paces. Over and over he paces and mumbles. Louder and louder his voice gets.

"Jules."

A loud shriek bubbles out of my throat as I jump up, ramming my head into Collin's chin in the process.

"Shit, Julie." He rubs my forehead while I blink and try to regain my senses. "I didn't mean to scare you. You okay?" His eyes fill with concern.

"Yeah. I had a nightmare is all." My brows furrow. "Did you win the game?"

Collin smiles. "Yeah. We won." His smile wavers a bit. "Do you want to talk about your nightmare?"

"No." Then I notice Deanna is gone. "Did Deanna leave?"

Collin nods. "Once I got here, she did. Let's go to bed. It's late and you're obviously ready."

I sit completely upright and it suddenly hits me what Deanna and I talked about. "Wait. Collin, we need to talk." He becomes very still, but waits for me. "I don't blame you. For telling me to leave and what happened after. It's not your fault." He opens his mouth, but I rest my forefinger over it. "Let it go, Collin. It doesn't matter in the grand scheme of things. I hadn't even thought about it until Deanna told me it still bothered you; that's how much it doesn't bother me. So, for me, let it go. Please?"

"For you," he says with a nod.

"Thank you."

Collin leans forward to kiss me softly. "Bed, Jules."

He stands, takes my hand, and leads me to his bedroom.

The next few minutes are bland as we prepare for bed. Collin keeps sneaking looks at me, but I'm unsure why.

"How are you feeling?" he asks as we crawl underneath the sheets.

"Okay."

"Can I hold you?"

What a crazy question. I snuggle against his side. The pure contentedness that comes from being held by someone who absolutely loves me is fulfilling. I'm right where I need to be. Where I belong.

As if reading my mind, Collin says, "Do you feel like we made it? Like we're finally where we belong? Like we overcame all we needed to and it'll be as smooth sailing as it can be from here on out?"

"Yeah, I do."

His sigh is one of relief. "I never thought I'd say it, but I'm ready for the season to be over. We will be spending so much time relaxing."

I chuckle. "You forget that I don't get summers off."

"We will still be relaxing, Jules. Just you and me."

"Where will Cal be?" I tease.

"Not my problem. It will be just us," he promises.

We fall quiet before the fact that I have a job hits me again. "When should I return to work?"

"Whenever you feel ready, Jules."

I accept that answer and close my eyes, praying for no nightmares.

175

"Isn't this a conflict of interest?"

Collin's therapist chuckles. "Would you like to see someone else?"

"No," I reply quietly, my eyes bouncing from spot to spot around the room. After a week of nightmares, Collin refused to leave for his road trip unless I promised to make an appointment with a therapist. So here I am with his own therapist. While I encouraged Collin to speak with someone, I feel so uncomfortable.

"Tell me how it feels to be home."

"Nice," I answer with a shrug. "I went back to work today. Everyone treats me as if I was gone on a horrible vacation." My gaze briefly lands on Mr. Lexington. "I feel like he's still out there somewhere."

He nods. "It can be hard to accept he's truly out of your life. You'll get there. Do you think that's part of why you're having nightmares?"

Well, he gets straight to the point.

"Maybe. He's been in my life in some way for such a long time. And now, poof." I wave my hands in the air. It almost doesn't make sense. It's impossible. Isn't it? "How am I supposed to break the habit of always looking over my shoulder? Or worrying when he'll take me again? Life is supposed to be normal after such a long period of abnormalcy?" I ask incredulously.

"One breath. One step. One day at a time, Julie."

That makes me roll my eyes.

"I'm serious. You're looking at the big picture and it's overwhelming. We need to look at the small picture. The current picture. Only what matters at this very second for the time being." When I give him a skeptical look, he dives further into this topic.

I do my best to listen and put my best foot forward, just as I wanted Collin to do. When I leave, I drive straight to the apartment, happy to be done with everything needed for the day. Somehow, Collin manages to text me, asking how things went. I give him a short answer, but promise to give more detail when we can actually talk.

I'm not sure if I feel any better after having my first official therapy session. But it's a start. It's the beginning of a new life. A new time when I can be as happy as I wish with only life's natural curveballs to cause disruptions. And that is something I can look forward to.

Collin

THE SERIES HAS us down three games to two as we enter game six. We're on foreign ice. The home crowd is roaring, eager and cheering on their team to finish us off tonight. There have been too many losses this year. I plan to get as many wins as I can, even if it means spending extra time away from home. Away from Julie.

Despite not having our own fans outweighing the home crowd, the energy within the locker room right before the game is to start is higher than it's been yet this playoff season. Maybe it's because we've made it as far as we have. Maybe it's because everything is on the line in this game tonight. Maybe it's because we're so damn hungry for the win. Either way, it's fuel for the fire.

The intensity is even higher the moment the puck touches the ice. The sounds of the game roar in my ears, filling my head. My blood pumps with an energy that can only be found during this time of year. Add in the natural anxiety I get and it's an odd type of high.

Up and down the ice we go. Shooting shot after shot at their goalie and holding our breaths when Savage is faced with a shot. Somehow, with all the back and forth and scrapping in front of the goalies, the first period ends without much action on the board.

The second period begins with a flurry of activity in front of both nets as a guy from each team gets called for a penalty. I'm on the bench when I see Rams score all the way from the blue line. The puck manages to fly through the air, over the goalie's head, bounces off his back, and into the net as the goalie inadvertently slides backward. But two minutes later, I'm on the ice, fighting an asshole of a player in the defensive zone, battling for the puck, when he manages to snag it away. He quickly passes it to his teammate who whips past my brother to make his shot.

And scores.

A few minutes later, Zane gets hit particularly rough and out of the blue. The puck left his stick about seven seconds before the hit, a clear thirty feet down the ice away from him, when he's checked hard into the boards by a player rushing across the ice. Everyone on the bench stands, breath stuck in our lungs as he lies on the ice for a second too long for comfort. Almost immediately, Brayden, who wasn't too far away, closes the distance. The gloves fly off his hands in one smooth motion. Our eyes bounce back and forth between the fight and Zane. He comes to his feet as the fighting duo slip and fall, refs pulling them apart immediately.

As if the energy wasn't high enough in the arena, there's now a constant buzz, a new edge. But it doesn't help us in any way. We fight with all we have, but it's just not enough. In the middle of the third, the other team scores twice to secure the win and their place in the next round.

That's it.

Season is over.

I don't know how it's possible, but I feel a new heaviness and lightness. A lightness that I can put this long, troublesome season behind me, but a heaviness that it ended without the ultimate prize, without us going as far as I wanted. It's not until we're back in the hotel for the night, with plans to fly home tomorrow, that I check my phone.

Julie: *I'm sorry.*

The text makes me smile.

Me: *It's okay. Just looking forward to coming home now.*

Julie: *Is it bad to say I'll be glad when you are? It's been a rough few days.*

Me: *You haven't mentioned that…*

Julie: *I didn't want to distract you.*

This is enough of a red flag for me to call her.

"What's wrong, Jules?"

Cal glances over at me; he's my roomie as usual.

He's nosy.

Julie sighs. "I've just been antsy. Trace has been pushing me kinda hard lately. I feel like I've been left alone," she admits softly.

"Jules," I whisper back as softly. My heart aches that she still struggles as much as she does. Not that I expect for her to heal so fast, but I feel like she's moving at a slower pace than anyone would like.

"I just miss you."

"I'll be home tomorrow," I remind her.

"I know. Is the team doing anything tonight?" she asks, clearly over the subject.

"I don't know; Cal and I are in the hotel room. I think we just plan on getting some sleep. Our flight is early."

Julie lets me talk to her for about thirty minutes. Once I'm satisfied she is in better spirits, we hang up to go to bed, especially since it's way later back home than it is here.

"She is still not doing so good?" Cal asks.

"No. Maybe she'll do better once I'm home and not set to go anywhere."

I walk into my apartment the next day and wonder how I missed the fact that Julie's car was in the parking deck. Because when I walk inside and into my bedroom, there she lies in bed asleep with Marmalade down by her feet. She didn't tell me that she would be here. Did she intend not to go into work? Do I wake her and ask? She's had so much trouble sleeping lately. I'd hate to disrupt some decent sleep when she might have actually called in.

I quietly place my bags on the floor and walk over to the nightstand. I pick up her phone and decide to snoop. There's no password, so it takes me two seconds to see that she texted her boss yesterday evening to say she just needed today off. I wonder why she didn't tell me? I place her phone down and leave the room. She should get all the sleep she can get.

It's so weird to have nothing to do in the foreseeable future. The time right after the season ends is a time I actually hate. My anxiety normally spikes because of there being this decompression period we're all expected to take. While decompression can be good for the soul, especially for someone like me, for some reason my anxiety rebels when it comes to a hockey season ending.

I like to have a bigger purpose and relaxing just isn't enough. While Julie rests, I decide to bide my time by searching for places we can travel this summer. We're going on a trip whether she believes me or not. She'll get the time off work one way or another. The question is where to go, when, and what all will we do?

About two hours, one trip booked later, Julie stumbles out of the bedroom.

"You didn't wake me up?" she asks with a frown as she comes to sit next to me.

"You needed the sleep."

She cuddles into my side. "I told my boss I needed the day off. I didn't want to spend the day working when you would be here. I needed this instead."

"What do you want to do today?"

"Absolutely nothing."

"Okay."

We spend the day being lazy. We take a trip to the grocery store. We watch TV. We spend time making love in bed. I tell Julie about our upcoming trip to Europe. We talk about random things, regular life things, our future, anything and everything. Julie seems better than last night. I'm hoping today will prove to actually do her good. I see Trace tomorrow and I'll admit that I plan to ask him about her. He more likely than not won't tell me anything, but it won't hurt to ask.

"Do you like seeing Trace?" I ask.

"Some times, I do."

I laugh, understanding her answer.

"Even though I struggle some still, I think he's help-ing."

That's a relief to hear. I'm not in her head, so I can't be absolutely sure how she's doing. Knowing that she thinks she's improving is great.

"He thinks I need to read the police report about what went down with Dwight."

"Why?" I ask, immediately outraged that he would send her mind back to that day.

"He thinks if I know, if I can picture how it happened, it'll give me some closure and the nightmares will stop."

I lack the optimism Trace seems to have about this, but I don't voice that. Julie watches and analyzes me for a moment.

"I want to do it."

"Okay." I nod in agreement. That one word, one ac-tion, seems to relax her, as if she was looking for permis-sion. As if she needed to know I was on her side and thought it was a good idea too, even though I don't think so, but I most definitely am on her side.

"He also thinks I should talk to my parents."

This is something I've been thinking about as well. I'm not too sure what went wrong with Julie and her parents, but she hasn't spoken to them since she kicked them out of her hospital room.

"Or at least tell him why I don't talk to them."

"What about tell me?" I ask hopefully.

That makes her smile, but for only a second. "I don't want to talk about it just yet."

"But you're doing better?"

She nods and I relax a little more.

I, myself, finally seem to be truly stabilizing. Questions and reports are still swirling about my mental health. Most players don't discuss these kinds of things until they retire. The team gives the same statement every time they are asked about it. I've been told the ball is in my court as far as if I would like to speak about it.

Cal has been curiously silent with his opinion. Julie is lost in her own issues. I'm undecided, which is a change from before when I knew I'd never speak of it. Possibly speaking out will be one of our topics of discussions in therapy tomorrow. Who knows? Maybe I'll come around and make this one of my missions to be an advocate for as well. That seems like a lot of pressure and a big decision. Once it's made, there's no going back.

"What are you thinking about?" Julie asks.

"Things I'm going to talk to Trace about tomorrow." When she quirks a smile, my eyes narrow. "What?"

"For someone so set against therapy, you sure do seem to look forward to it now."

I gently nudge my elbow into her stomach. "Leave me alone; no one ever said I was the smartest Kessy."

She laughs and it's the greatest sound I've heard to-day.

23

Julie

"**D**O YOU WANT to discuss your parents first or read the report?"

They both sound like horrible ideas. However, the issue with my parents will be less traumatic, so I choose them.

"I know why you don't have anything to do with your sister, but you haven't really explained what happened in the hospital room or why you don't want anything to do with your parents right now. Let's hear it." Trace leans back in his seat and waits.

Three words. Three words weigh down so heavily on my tongue I'm not sure I can bear to say them aloud. I don't want to admit it. I don't want to believe it. I want to keep ignoring it in the way that I have. But if I want to put this mess with Dwight behind me, then I need to take this step.

"It's their fault," I whisper.

"What is their fault?"

"Dwight."

Trace understandably looks confused.

"I asked him why he met me and he said…" I close my eyes and shake my head. "It was my parents. He told me some elaborate story about how he met my dad and then saw a picture of me. He conned them into giving him all the information he needed to run into me and it snowballed from there. They even once suggested how they should set us up on a date." A gag involuntarily emits from my throat. "They had a part in this," I mutter, completely heartbroken.

"And then, they walked into that hospital room, acting as if they cared, and all I could think was they gave him what he needed to know. They are the reason he found me in North Carolina!" I shout, unable to hold in my outrage any longer. "He called them," I explain, tears flowing down my cheeks. "He said that we had been secretly dating, but I got mad and took off. He asked where I might go and they told him about Collin. I could've been safe if not for them. I could've been safe." As those last four words leave my mouth, I completely break down into sobs.

Trace gets up. I don't know what happens, so lost in my crying, but a moment later, a pair of arms wrap around me.

"Jules, it's okay," Collin whispers. A feeling of safety immediately engulfs me. "It's okay," he repeats. "What happened?"

"Can I tell him?" I hear Trace ask when it's clear nothing but jibber emits from my own mouth. All I can do is nod. I can't say those words again. I do what I can to block out the sound of Trace telling Collin, who Trace apparently wanted on standby for my inevitable breakdown.

"Jules," Collin says softly when the story is complete. "Can you imagine how they feel right now knowing what happened to you because of the information they provided?"

I lift my head from his shoulder and glare at him.

He rests a finger over my mouth. "They are your parents, Julie. They didn't know. Had they known, you know as good as I do that they never would have put you in danger like that. You need to talk to them. I'm sure they want to apologize."

"I'm not going back." I'm *never* going back to Florida for as long as I live.

"That's why we have planes for them to come here and cell phones for when no one wants to go anywhere, Julie," he says with a slight tease in his tone. "Think about it." He kisses me softly and that ends the discussion. I know it. He knows it. Even Trace seems to know it.

"Do you still want to read the report or is that enough for today?"

"Let's get it over with."

Collin stands to leave, but I grab his hand.

"Don't go."

He nods and takes a seat in the chair next to me.

Trace hands over the police report. It rests in my hands for what seems like forever before I begin to read their account of what happened that day.

There was a tip about the neighbor speaking to a man looking a lot like Dwight and she reported hearing a lot of yelling as well. They sent a team out to investigate, prepared for the worst since they suspected I was in Florida anyway. They shouted their presence, heard a noise inside that sounded like running. They busted the front and back doors open and that's when Dwight, faced with officers at all vantage points, opened fire.

He was shot multiple times by the officers and was dead before the tape was removed from my mouth. Dwight was just out of sight from where I was and it appears an officer had enough time to make it to the couch, which wasn't too far from the back door. The officer that removed the tape from my mouth is the one who apparently stood so that if Dwight fired toward me, he'd have a hard time hitting anything other than the officer's body.

I read the report two more times, reading about things they found, skipping the parts about my own condition. Peace slowly fills my body along with an overwhelming gratitude toward the officer.

"Julie?"

I glance up to look at Trace.

"How are you feeling?"

"Better."

Trace smiles. "Good. Do you want to discuss anything?"

I shake my head. "No. I'd like to go home."

His eyes widen in surprise and he opens his mouth to object, but Collin cuts him off.

"It's been a long session, Trace. She's like me. She knows when she's had enough. We'll take it easy at home and maybe you can call her parents in the next session."

This time it's me who wants to object, but Trace interrupts me. This session just keeps turning on its head. Collin escorts me out of the building and doesn't even talk about what happened. Instead, he says that he's working with the team's PR people because he does want to speak out about his anxiety. He wants to figure out how to make this be a good thing, but also work for him both short-term and long-term.

That's enough of a show stopper, though I thought he was leaning toward that, that I can't help but dive into a discussion with him. I'm one step closer on this long road of healing, but I can't help but think I'm not close to the end.

It's a Thursday in late May when someone knocks on the door while Collin is out at the grocery store. Who could possibly be coming over? Marmalade jumps onto the back of the recliner and watches me walk over to the door.

"Hey, Deanna. Should I be expecting you?" I ask cautiously, searching my mind for some missed plans.

"No. Grab your purse. We have plans."

"I have to get to work."

Deanna shakes her head. "Collin went over your head and you are off until next week. Now go."

"Why?" I ask without moving a muscle. Collin doesn't like surprises for himself, but he likes to give me surprises.

"Trust me for once and do as I've asked."

Since Collin is behind this, I decide her request isn't

unreasonable. Thirty minutes later, we're in a nearby town that I haven't really explored yet. We pull into a shopping center and I'm confused further when I see Collin, Cal, and Brayden standing in front of one of the stores.

Collin walks over by the time I've opened my door and stepped out of the car. "Collin, what is going on?"

"You'll see."

He leads me away from our friends to a courtyard-like area and stops underneath a weeping willow. He's starting to worry me. Collin faces me and takes a deep breath.

"Jules." For a moment, that is the only word between us. It hangs in the air, flowing back and forth with the breeze. "I love you. I've loved you for a long time. Being with you is more than I ever could've asked out of life. Things are a challenge for us, but loving one another has never been a challenge. It's easy. It's perfect. And it's because we belong together." He takes a deep, now shaky breath. "I say all of this to ask if you'll marry me?" He falls to one knee and plucks a ring from his pocket.

The diamonds glint from the sunlight filtering through the hanging foliage. My brain is stuck on the *marry me* part while my eyes are glued to the ring. I don't think any of this is processing. Am I even awake? Maybe I'm dreaming.

"Jules," Collin whispers. "You better say something before I get to a thirteen."

"You're serious?"

He doesn't laugh. He doesn't smile. He doesn't find my question at all amusing, which is good because I'm serious, too. Instead, he nods and says, "As serious as the worst of what we've been through. We're catching up, remember?"

"Yes," I answer both of his questions.

His brows furrow slightly. "Yes?"

"Yes, let's get married."

Collin grins, stands, and kisses me hard. A few hoots and hollers can be heard in the background. Collin stops kissing me long enough to slip my new, beautiful ring onto my finger before going in for another kiss.

"So," he begins once our kissing session is completed. "Can we get married this weekend?" My eyes pop. "You can pick out a dress today with Deanna; I'll get a tux. We'll get our marriage license and then we'll have a small ceremony Saturday before taking our honeymoon next week. It's all planned if you're ready."

I've never been more ready for anything in my life, even though I wasn't expecting it at all. It's funny how life works out sometimes. Marrying Collin was nowhere on my radar, yet here we are and I couldn't be happier about it. Although, all of his talks about the future lately make a lot more sense.

We've been through so much, individually and together. Our journey to this point was a long one, but it was worth it. Being together where we belong is all the guarantee I need that our future, no matter how low the downs are, will be satisfying, fulfilling, and full of so much love.

When I turn around this time, to face our friends, our parents are now standing with them.

"It's time, Julie," Collin says softly.

My parents have joined me via phone for a few sessions with Trace and we've made some progress, but to see them here?

I didn't know how I'd feel. It's why I kept pushing

my parents off when they asked if they could come visit. I didn't think I would be prepared for it. But I find myself not only happy to see them, but relieved. Part of me wants to act like a little girl and run over for a hug. Instead, Collin and I walk over to everyone. With tears already falling down my face, I throw my arms around the necks of my parents.

"I'm sorry," I cry.

"You have nothing to be sorry for," Mom says.

"Thank you for not asking us to leave," Dad says.

"We can stay, can't we?" Mom asks.

I pull back and nod. "I'd be happy if you did." Things aren't as awkward as I thought they'd be. The negative emotions that I thought would overrun me aren't there.

"Shall we split up and start shopping?" Deanna asks. "Julie needs a dress."

And it hits me what I've said yes to. What will be happening this weekend. My gaze finds Collin who smiles.

That feeling I had when I came to North Carolina and kissed him? That feeling of the world finally being righted? I feel it again now. We are exactly where we belong.

Acknowledgements

Thank you, Kristalyn Thornock. You stand by me no matter what. Thank you for your patience!

Thank you, Angie Wells, for being a beta reader for me! Your feedback has proven time and time again to be so valuable and I don't know what I would do without your help.

Thank you, Shannon Page. You fix my errors and help me put out a work I can be proud of.

Thank you, Robin from Wicked by Design. Your work is always beautiful!

Thank you, Julie from JT Formatting, for always making time for me!

Thank you, reader, for being patient and waiting for this story. I hope you love it as much as I do.

ABOUT THE AUTHOR

LINDSAY PAIGE IS the author of multiple Young Adult, New Adult, and Sports romances. She also enjoys writing books with characters who deal with anxiety and depression, issues which are close to her heart. Lindsay is a North Carolinian who loves watching hockey, having conversations with her two dogs, rewatching episodes of M*A*S*H, and living her dream of writing books for a living.

If you would like to hear news before anyone else, interact with Lindsay, and have a place to discuss her books with fellow fans, join Lindsay's League on Facebook.

https://www.facebook.com/groups/lindsaysleague/

Author Links:

Website:
lindsaypaige.com

Facebook:
facebook.com/authorlindsaypaige

Facebook Group:
https://www.facebook.com/groups/lindsaysleague/

Instagram:
https://www.instagram.com/authorlindsaypaige/

Newsletter Sign Up:

Stay up-to-date on books, news, sales, and giveaways by
signing up for her monthly newsletter!
http://eepurl.com/hqcTw

Coming Soon

Lindsay Paige is stepping outside of her comfort zone with her next book; stay tuned for more details!

Carolina Rebels Roster:

No.	Name	Nickname	Position
1	Collin Kessy	Thing 1	Center
2	Cal Kessy	Thing 2	Right Wing
7	Scott Boyd	Scotty	Right Wing
10	Tommy Alderson	Tommy Boy	Left Wing
11	Luukas Lathi	Luck	Center
13	Brayden Hayes	Captain Hook	Center
17	Ross Strome	Rossy	Defenseman
19	Marc Polinski	Marco Polo	Defenseman
20	Elias Bertuzzi	EJ	Center
24	Noah Ramsey	Rams	Defenseman
26	Dylan Copley	Po Po	Defenseman
30	Sergey Orlovsky	Serge	Left Wing
32	Kellan Hellberg	Hells	Center
37	Liam Irving	Savage/Sav	Goalie
41	Reid Aubry	Soda	Defenseman
44	Eric Kelly	Kel	Goalie
46	Tyler Lindberg	Lindy	Right Wing

58	Bradley Potter	Pots	Left Wing
62	Kyle McNally	Nally	Left Wing
68	Zane Landry	Z	Defenseman
74	Nathan O'Donnell	Donny	Right Wing
85	Ian Rhett	Bruiser	Defenseman
94	Jeffery Olsen	Olsey	Right Wing

Lindsay has written the following books/series:

Bending Under Pressure

Bold as Love series

Bracing for Love series

Carolina Rebels series

Don't Panic

Sanity series

Without a Doubt

You Before Me

She has cowritten the following series:

The Penalty Kill Trilogy

Oh Captain, My Captain series

The Ninth Inning series

www.ingramcontent.com/pod-product-compliance
Lightning Source LLC
Chambersburg PA
CBHW060932180626
46817CB00004B/1511